"I'm afraid," she whispered.

"Are you disappointed in me?"

"Perhaps. I'd rather not talk about it."

"Then don't," she whispered fiercely. Her arms were tight about him and she burrowed closer against his body under the blankets. The animal movements she now made were obvious in their intent.

Why not? he thought. *The past was dead.*

"Sam?" she said.

There was no need to reply.

His pulse quickened and then there was the silk of her body pressing against him, stirring and waking him.

Her lips pressed with avid hunger against his.

Other Fawcett Gold Medal Books in the "Assignment" Series
by Edward S. Aarons:

Assignment • • • • •

BUDAPEST

EDWARD S. AARONS

A FAWCETT GOLD MEDAL BOOK

Fawcett Publications, Inc., Greenwich, Connecticut
Member of American Book Publishers Council, Inc.

Chapter One

DURELL did not get into it until three hours after it began. Matt Breagan was called first, out of the Trenton office, at six o'clock on that January morning. A fine skin of ice glittered on the Limekiln Road where he drove to meet McEneny. By then, everything was coming loose between Jersey and Washington. Breagan did what he could, but it wasn't enough, and even though the matter lay within the jurisdiction of the FBI, he called in Durell. But that was three hours later.

McEneny's sedan was parked near the junction of Limekiln and a nameless farm lane that curved over the flat Jersey fields. Two state patrol cars were also parked here, but Breagan went to join McEneny first. To the south, a long line of armed men in hats, coats and boots moved in a slow, plodding search toward a growth of scrub pine and pin oak woods. Dawn was two hours past, and the winter sky was the color of slate, heavy and oppressive, streaked an ochrous yellow in the east. The wind was close to forty an hour, Breagan estimated. And, he thought, if the murdering bastards are still out in this weather, they'll freeze to death. And that would save a lot of people a bad headache.

But he had small hope that that would happen.

Breagan had had time only for coffee, and his bones felt cold and brittle, and his flesh shivered under his blue overcoat. He was nearly fifty, head of the field office in Trenton, a widower with a son at Princeton, not far away. He was getting old for this sort of thing, he kept thinking, and he wondered with a silent fury how it could have happened at all, how the man could have been ferried from Vienna to the reception center at Kilmer with all the other Hungarian refugees, and then make his break from there.

The long line of armed men moved like ants across the flat, snowy fields and were gradually eaten up by the broken outline of the pine woods. One of the state police cars at the road intersection started up and drove away toward New Brunswick. A trooper from the other car stood out in the wind, a stubby automatic rifle in his gauntleted hand. The man's face looked blue with cold under his fur helmet. Breagan conjured up in his mind a quick, competent map of the area and spotted himself at this road junction. A radius of over five miles from where Bela Korvuth was last seen. One hell of an area to cover. It wasn't really possible. They could slip through, or hide out somewhere, in a barn, a shed, a gully or culvert; they could double back toward New Brunswick and hop a bus, a train, or lift a car and take off toward New York or Philadelphia. There weren't enough men to close the perimeter of this circle tight enough. There were never enough men. Still, you had to try to slam the cork into the bottle somehow; that was your job.

McEneny nodded as Breagan got into the car with him. He was talking quietly on the radio phone to somebody on the opposite side of the perimeter. How many houses, how many people, how many roads, lanes, paths, in and out of this frozen area? The weather might help. It was really their only chance to nip this thing before it got away from them. And the newspapers—dear Christopher, Breagan thought, what a field day the newsmen will have!

There had been enough rumors about enemy agents slipping into Kilmer along with the flood of thousands upon thousands of innocent refugees from Hungary. None of them had checked out to anything. The filtering and screening was as tight as man could make it. Yet it had happened this morning, and with no one less than Bela Korvuth. It was like learning that someone had let loose a plague.

McEneny cradled his radio phone and looked at him. "You look beat, Matt. Are you all right?"

"I'm disgusted," Breagan said.

"I've been talking to Colonel Morsham at the camp." McEneny was a good-looking, well-fed young man, with bland blue eyes and a mild manner and a mind as quick and devious as any ambulance-chasing lawyer. He was also the crack shot of the Trenton office. "Morsham's pants are getting wet," McEneny said. "He's asking us for God's sake to stop Bela Korvuth now. Right now."

"How did he get in there in the first place?"

"He came through with the last batch of refugees from Vienna. Morsham doesn't know how he slipped through the screening."

"He's got to know," Breagan said angrily. His fury still goaded him. "Korvuth is like a time bomb, loose in this country. If he was mugged and printed and checked out with all the others, then somebody covered for him."

"Looks that way. A rat in the woodpile. One of our own people, I'd say." McEneny looked angry, too, for a moment. "Korvuth couldn't have made it otherwise. Of course, he isn't alone, as I told you on the phone, Matt. He went over the fence at the reception center with another man and the woman who came over as his wife. We've got them all tagged now—closing the barn door after the old mare is stolen. The other man is named Zoltan Ske. Mean anything to you?"

"He was a colonel in the Hungarian AVO."

"Check. The woman posing as Korvuth's wife is Ilona Nebro. The same name Korvuth used. All three took off when Morsham nailed down the faked check reports from Vienna. I guess they were tipped it was coming, or expecting it, anyway. They moved fast when they saw Morsham and his M.P.'s enter the barracks. Morsham's mistake. He let them see him first. God knows how they did it, but they got away." McEneny chuckled.

"It's not funny, Harry."

"They took Morsham's staff car, that's what. Ditched it five miles from here, at a farm owned by some people named Dunstermeir. They came into his house to warm up, he says, and took his rifle—a Remington .30-08, a twelve-gauge shotgun, and a Luger pistol."

"Dear God," Breagan said. "Quite an armory."

"And then the three of them—Bela, Zoltan Ske, and the woman—tied up Mr. Dunstermeir and took off in his truck. Fifty-four Chevrolet, red stake-body. I've got the license number here. By then we had the check points up on the road and we know damned well they haven't slipped through yet. They're somewhere inside this circle, all right."

"You're an optimist."

"They won't get away, Matt."

Breagan sighed. "They're already away."

Breagan and McEneny drove to meet Colonel Morsham, halfway around the search perimeter. No thought of Durell had yet occurred to Breagan; there was no reason to connect Durell with this, and no reason, particularly in view of the jealously guarded departmental jurisdictions, to call upon State or the CIA. It was after eight o'cock in the morning, and a fine spit of snow began to cover the flat fields and scrubby woods of the New Jersey midlands. There was little traffic on the roads. They passed through two check points manned by the state police, who were cooperating in every possible way. Another barrier was run by Morsham's M.P.'s. The cold weather was hindering the search as well as helping to pin down the fugitives. The wind was sharper, and the snow slanted in almost horizontal lines across the white fields.

Colonel Morsham was in a construction shack by the Turnpike, standing near a potbellied iron stove that roared and glowed cherry-red with the fire of kindling and scrap lumber. Two Army jeeps, a command car, and a state patrol cruiser were parked outside, and McEneny's sedan skidded a little on the thickening ice as he pulled up in front of the shack.

Morsham was a stout man in his late forties, red-faced, with prematurely white hair and a small white military mustache. He was the perfect pattern of Colonel Blimp, Breagan reflected, and from past contact with the man he knew that Morsham had been in the Army long enough to know how to pass the buck upward, but not quite long enough to be able to shrug off all sense of responsibility. The shack was crowded, with a couple of non-coms at a field radio and a state trooper near the roaring stove. Breagan nodded, wishing he could stay near the fire to stop his shivering, but he decided there were too many men here now, and he beckoned Morsham outside into the lee of the construction shack, where they could talk alone and freely. McEneny stayed inside.

"I've called Washington," Morsham said. "It's a kick in the teeth. They told me to turn everything over to you, Breagan. It's in your lap now, and I can't deny I'm glad to get it off my hands. Naturally, we're going to cooperate in every possible way. You can have all the men and equipment you need. It's chancy, but this Korvuth man and his companions may still be within the area."

"No trace of the truck they stole from the farm?"

"Nothing. Probably they're holed up in some barn. With this snow, of course, they'll leave tracks if they move at all. I've got two platoons coming from Signal, up north. The state police are pulling in more cars every minute. I think we'll find them, all right."

"What else did Washington say, besides handing me the baby?" Breagan asked.

"They're already rolling on the other side of the line, checking back in Austria to the people who screened these Hungarians we got in the last batch. The trouble started over there, of course. Not here. After all, I only get these people after they've been screened and double-checked."

"Nobody blames you for that," Breagan said. "But you were damned careless letting Korvuth see your M.P.'s coming."

"We thought he was still asleep. I wasn't with those men, mind you. Matter of fact, I was still—"

"It's all right," Breagan said. He didn't want to hear any of Morsham's alibis. The damage was already done. "There's nothing to do now but tighten the net and see what we find."

"Who is this Bela Korvuth, anyway?" Morsham asked. His red face was even redder now, with the wind sliding around the corner of the shack to cut at them. His pale eyes watered, and his nose looked wet. Breagan kept shuddering inside his overcoat. "What's so important about the man? Washington didn't brief me on him at all."

Breagan felt a coldness that went beyond the bitter morning weather. He thought about it for a moment and decided there was no harm in letting Morsham know something of what he was up against.

"Bela Korvuth is only a name to us. He was a general in the Hungarian secret police, the AVO; but he was more than that, too. We've got his pictures now, thanks to the screening, but we've heard a lot about him for the past couple of years. He's the Soviet hatchet man par excellence. He makes Machiavelli and the Borgias look like two-bit clumsy pikers."

"I don't understand," Morsham said uneasily.

Breagan's voice was sharp. "The man is an assassin. Washington thinks he's responsible for the disappearance of half a dozen dissenters within the Communist hierarchy lately. Killing is his business. He's clever about it, too. Never works the same way twice—and most of the deaths he's brought about, among satellite and even Russian big brass, have been filed under all sorts of reasons, but none of them as murder."

"I think I see," Morsham muttered. He looked away at the bleak expanse of fields behind the construction shack. "But why would Bela Korvuth slip into this country, if his job is that of an intra-party hatchet man?"

"Maybe he's expanding his field," Breagan said drily.

"I don't really see—"

"He must be here to assassinate somebody," Breagan said. He turned away, back toward the shack door, and Morsham stood looking after him with eyes suddenly bright with ugly knowledge. Breagan tossed his last words over his shoulder. "His intended victim could be anybody from the very top all the way down the line."

Half an hour at the temporary headquarters in the shack was enough for Breagan. Nothing was happening. The perimeter around the search area had closed in here and there, with the search of scattered and isolated farms, but nothing had turned up. Korvuth, Zoltan Ske, and the woman had vanished into thin air, or burrowed into the ground. Breagan had no illusions about himself. He knew that in spite of all his own training, he was up against an opponent who could probably play rings around him.

"Let's talk to this farmer, Dunstermeir," he said.

McEneny drove. The farm was off beyond several snowy fields and a thick stand of second-growth soft maples, with a red dairy barn and a shining aluminum silo and a Victorian farmhouse painted a pristine, silvery white. The place looked as if someone cared for it, worked on it, and loved it. McEneny had left a man, Frank Orzanski, with Dunstermeir and his wife. Orzanski reported nothing new.

"No word from the truck?" Breagan asked.

"Nothing yet. This is Mr. Dunstermeir. And his wife."

They were frightened. They were trying not to show it, but the fear was there, flickering behind the couple's pale blue eyes. They looked more like brother and sister than husband and wife, regular Grant Wood characters, Breagan thought, with implacable faces stamped with years of close association with the soil, with the struggle for crops and battles against weather and insects and market prices. The house shone cleanly inside just as the farm buildings and equipment were cared for outside. The rooms were all furnished with the tasseled and rococo elegance of another age and time. A bowed-glass cabinet in the living room gave Breagan a glimpse of a fine collection of Meissen china, and somehow he was not surprised by this.

Breagan spoke gently against the fear here. "It's all right, now. Just tell us what happened."

"I have already told this man," Dunstermeir said.

"Tell it again."

The farmer was thin, with wispy gray hair, a rather long nose, and a harsh, lipless mouth. His wife, equally angular, stood with her hands folded under her apron, a step behind him in the big country kitchen. A huge pot of soup bubbled on the old iron coal stove.

"They came in this Army car," Dunstermeir said. He spoke with just a faint German accent. "They said they wanted to make a telephone call. And the next thing I know, they have my guns, the two men. The woman, she said nothing. She looks frightened. They ask for my truck, the new one in the barn. I was frightened by the smaller man. There was something terrible about the way he acted. I remember—twenty years ago, in Nazi Germany, when we saw the trouble coming and Hilda and I decided to get out— he was something like those men who killed and looted and dragged people from bed at night—"

"Take it easy," Breagan said again.

"So I do what they demand," Dunstermeir said thinly. "Nothing more or less. I did not want to be hurt. I did not want Hilda hurt. We obeyed. We gave them what they wanted."

"Just the truck?"

"Some food. Fifty dollars. And they used the telephone."

Breagan looked at McEneny. "You're checking that?"

"Johnson is looking into it. It's a rural party line. We'll find out who and where," McEneny said.

"All right." Breagan spoke to Dunstermeir. "Did they say anything more to you? Give you any idea who they were and what they wanted?"

"They asked for the truck. They made Endre go with them."

"Who is Endre?"

McEneny said, "The hired hand. Young fellow, one of the Hungarians. The Dunstermeirs took him in out of the first batch."

Breagan and McEneny looked at each other, both thinking the same thing. He asked the farmer: "Where is Endre now?"

"He is not yet back. Nor is the truck."

There was something wrong here. Breagan had been in the business long enough to learn not to discount intuitive hunches completely. Dunstermeir looked away from him when he tried to meet the man's eye. The fear in this couple went beyond the immediate incident that had shaken their lives. It was something deeper and more fundamental. It could have been caused by old memories and a revival of half-forgotten terrors that had brought them here originally; but Breagan did not think so. There was an immediacy to the fear he smelled in this house now.

He lit a cigarette, took off his hat, and brushed back his thick gray hair. He found the warmth of the kitchen welcome, but none of his tiredness eased up. Through the windows he saw the thin, sleety snow flying every which way in the dooryard between the house and the dairy barn. Nothing moved out there to disturb the Currier and Ives aspect of this place. It was almost too perfect, Breagan thought, in its nostalgic reconstruction of a more peaceful time. Maybe that was it. The place and the Dunstermeirs were too good to be true. McEneny, with his bland, quick mind, hadn't seen it, obviously, although he had caught some of Breagan's disturbed reservations.

"What exactly did Bela Korvuth say to you?" Breagan asked quietly.

"I do not know which one was Korvuth," Dunstermeir said.

"The leader. The one in charge."

"The smaller man? The one who frightened Mama?"

"That's probably he," Breagan said, nodding. "Didn't he say anything out of line at all?"

Dunstermeir and his wife exchanged a quick glance, and Breagan felt a quickening in him. There was something here, all right. He forgot the way he had been wakened at dawn to get out into this frozen morning. But he didn't rush it. When the woman offered him a cup of coffee, he accepted quietly, his manner gentle, knowing McEneny, too, felt it at last, and was waiting for his move.

"What else did Korvuth say?" Breagan insisted.

The woman spoke. "He took Endre with him. Endre recognized him—perhaps from the fighting in Budapest. They took the guns. I felt sorry for the girl. She looked nice. She was afraid of him."

"Are you sure of that?"

"It is a feeling I had. And then Korvuth told us—"

"Hilda, be quiet," the man said.

"But he ordered us to tell these men!" she insisted. "And we should. You say it is none of our business, but we should, Papa."

It was too good, too pat, this little quarrel between them.

It might have been a clever bit of play-acting. Breagan wasn't sure. He still rode his intuition, and he still kept his voice gentle, as if he knew them and trusted them and understood their fears.

"Go on, Mrs. Dunstermeir. It may be important. Do I get you right, that Korvuth gave you a message for us?"

"For a man named Durell," the woman said.

"Sam Durell?"

"A man in Washington by that name, yes."

"What exactly did Korvuth say?"

The Dunstermeirs exchanged another quick look. The fear wasn't there any more. Something else glittered in the pale blue eyes that watched Breagan's heavy, tired movement across the kitchen. Was it triumph? Violence? Hatred? He wasn't sure. He could be imagining all of it.

The woman spoke quietly.

"Korvuth said he came to this country to kill two men. He wanted the police—the CIA, he said—to know that. He would not name one of the men. But the other he named. It was Durell."

McEneny made a small, vague sound and looked at Breagan. "Isn't he the one who worked with our New York office on the Stella Marni case?"

"Yes," Breagan said.

"We've got to let him know."

Breagan exhaled softly. He found that his hands were clenched at his sides, and Mr. Dunstermeir was looking at them, aware of the explosive impact of his words. But the farmer's stony face gave nothing away now. I'm getting too old for this, Breagan thought again. Too old and tired, when a man like this can read me so easily.

"I'll call Washington," he said quietly.

Chapter Two

DURELL put the telephone away and walked down the hall back to Deirdre. A thin rain was falling, turning the Chesapeake, glimpsed beyond the village of Prince John, in Maryland, into a dimpled plate of sullen gray steel. It was ten-thirty on that Saturday morning. He had driven over from

Washington for breakfast with Deirdre Padgett, with a long winter's weekend ahead of them, alone here, just the two of them. That was gone now, but he didn't let the disappointment trouble him after the first few moments.

"It was Dickinson McFee," he said to Deirdre, and sat down at the table again.

"Do you have to go?" she asked quietly.

"Yes. There will be a plane at the local airport soon. We have half an hour."

"Oh, Sam . . ."

"Forget it, hon," he said. "Where were we?"

"What does it matter?" Her words were toneless. "We could talk about it forever, and nothing would materialize out of it. One phone call from your little general, and all the talk in the world between us goes up in smoke and remains just that—idle, wishful thinking. Talk, smoke, nothing at all."

"I'm sorry."

"I suppose I shouldn't ask where you're going, or why."

He smiled. "You know I wouldn't tell you."

"Yes, I know. I know it only too well."

He watched her fill his coffee cup again. The kitchen of this fine old Maryland house was quiet and peaceful. A small fire that he had built burned cheerfully in the red brick fireplace set into the kitchen wall, opposite the modern stove and the shining antique copperware that Deirdre loved. Through the twelve-over-twelve windows, he could see the sweep of wet lawn from the house to the water's edge. A man was out there in the chill rain, dredging for Chincoteagues from an ancient, dirty-white pungy in a cove of the bay, just north of the beach here. Durell knew the ways of the bay oystermen, in their bugeyes and pungies, and there was nothing really unusual about a crew of two or three going out in this weather. But he saw only one man, bent over on the narrow deck, forward of the small pilothouse. He wondered if it meant anything, and he sat very quietly while he considered it, his suspicion and alertness silencing him for the moment.

He was a tall man, black of hair, just over thirty, with a small dark mustache and a taut, competent mouth. His blue eyes often appeared black when he was angry or especially thoughtful. They were very dark just now. There was a fine coordination in the way his lean body moved. His hot Cajun temperament had been carefully honed and controlled by the years of his training and silent warfare he had experienced since his boyhood in the Louisiana bayous, far from this place. It had been necessary to learn that often the difference between the quick and the dead was patience, silence, and watchfulness. A long series of ghosts, of dead men he had once known and worked with, were grim evidence of the price one paid for a mistake or a miscalculation. The war that Durell fought was not one that rang with bugles or trembled to the beat of drums. It was dark and silent, fought with nerve and skill; the war of espionage; and its battlefield was only too often the dirty streets and black slum alleys of faraway corners of the troubled world. The weapons of this war were more often cunning and vigilance rather than strength, although occasionally knife or gun came into swift, explosive play. The years in which Durell had served in this war had left their mark upon him in indefinable ways. He had survived until now, when so many others had failed or broken or died, and this spoke for itself as to what he was and what he had become.

Deirdre saw him watching the man in the pungy.

"It's only old Tom Yordie," she said quietly.

"From Prince John?"

"He's been around ever since I was a child. He's perfectly harmless." Deirdre sighed. "You never relax, do you, darling? What is it with you? A perfectly fine old man, who's never missed a day oystering in his life, and you look at him with such suspicion. How long does such dedication to your job go on?"

"I can't afford to relax, Dee," he told her.

"Well, that's what I mean," she said.

He looked away from the fisherman in the cove. "It's too late for me," he said. "I can't get out of it now. It's all I know."

"And is it too late for me? For us? Look at me, Sam. Is it?"

He saw her in all her quiet, solemn loveliness, the one woman who had broken through his barriers and touched the emotions he thought he had buried and forgotten. He knew women better than most men, loved them and used them and forgot them. Deirdre Padgett was quite different. She had reached something in him that he had tried to destroy, and breathed life back into it; and sometimes he was sorry about this, not for himself, but for her, because there was no answer to the question she was asking him.

She got up and moved toward the brick kitchen fireplace.

Her back was straight and slim, her fine hips pliant and curved under the soft jersey dress she wore. Her dark black hair shone with luster in the gray morning light. Her eyes were somber. He had been attracted originally by the inner peace and composure she possessed, by the tranquillity of her, some of which he had destroyed by allowing their relationship to reach this point. He knew her as intimately as any man could know a woman. There were no secrets between them, except those of his profession, and it was this that constantly created a barrier between them that no amount of patience or understanding could overcome.

She spoke with her back to him. "Did you talk to McFee about me yesterday?"

"Of course. But I didn't tell him I would resign. I can't do that, Dee. I've been in this game too long, and I'm getting old in it."

"Like an old fox, or a wolf, in the wilderness."

"Yes, it's a wilderness, all right," he admitted.

She turned now to look directly at him. "But you love it, don't you, old fox?"

"It's my job. I love you, too, Dee."

"But never the twain shall meet," she said.

"It wouldn't be fair to you if we married," he told her. "Not to you or me or to McFee."

"Does he come into our private life, too?"

"He comes into everything. I couldn't do my job properly then. Not if I had to worry about you and know how you were worrying, too."

"But you know I'm willing to accept all that," she said tightly. "I don't want you to become a machine, like some of the others. Always suspicious, always living under some sort of cover personality so that sometimes when we're together and I look for you, I see someone else, not you, someone you make yourself into for the job. And I don't know that someone at all."

"It has to be that way. It's a question of survival."

"I know all that, too," she said. She came back to the table, picked up the silver coffee pot, looked at it, and put it down again. Durell was still watching the oysterman in the pungy. A touch of sleet hissed against the windows beside the dining table. The Chesapeake looked cold and ominous, and he suddenly held in his mind, for just an instant, the vignette of Bayou Peche Rouge, hot in the steaming sunlight, dark and secretive and green, all mysterious and wonderful in his boyhood. He watched a fish-hawk float into a small grove of pines near the point to the north.

Deirdre said: "Sam, I love you. It's just that I want to share everything with you. Didn't you ask McFee about a job for me?"

"No. I don't want you in it."

"That's for me to decide," she pointed out. "I could work with you, and—"

"No. Never." There was suppressed violence in him.

"Why not?"

He looked at her and wanted her and cherished her and felt the grievous sadness of the pain he constantly gave her. He wished he could be free to stay with her this weekend, here in this peaceful old house, just the two of them alone, to make love and talk of things remote from his work.

"Don't you know what might happen, Dee?" he said. "There might come a time and a place whan I would have to drop you. Abandon you, sooner or later, in some crisis or emergency. Or you might have to leave me somewhere, with no way out. To die, you understand?"

Her face was pale. "I couldn't do that to you."

"But I would, to you," he said harshly. "I'd have to. And if you wanted to live in this game, you'd have to do the same to me."

"No," she said. "No, no."

He stood up. "There you are. That's what I mean."

Deirdre searched his lean, dark face and shivered and hugged herself as if she had suddenly gone cold because of what she saw in him. She was so beautiful that he ached all over for her.

At that moment there came a sharp, snapping report from outside the quiet house. Durell's move was so swift and fluid that Deirdre was hardly aware of his movement as such at all, until he was at the window, a bit to one side, with his hand in his pocket.

It was only a backfire from the pungy's engine in the cove. He did not relax.

"You're jumpy, Sam. What is it? What did McFee want?"

"I've got to find a man," he said. "Someone got loose in the country. He's got to be found, fast."

"Or what?"

"Or he'll kill somebody. Somebody very important." *And Korvuth will try for you, too,* Durell thought. But he didn't tell her that. "I'll have to leave you now, hon," he said.

"I suppose there is no point in asking you to be careful," she whispered.

"I do what has to be done. It's my job," he said.

Dickinson McFee was at the little airport two miles west of the town of Prince John. The rain was colder, half sleet now, and the trees in the grim gray daylight were beginning to glimmer with a thin coating of ice. A four-seater Beach liaison plane, with private registry markings, was waiting for him. Durell did not know the pilot. He met General McFee in a small shelter hut a short distance from the battered old hangar.

"Sorry to break up your weekend like this, Sam." McFee looked tired, a small erect man of gray, with a mouth and voice possessed of the incisive quality of a steel trap. "I hope Deirdre didn't mind too much. Did you tell her I gave a negative on her application?"

"Yes. Thanks."

"All right, then. I have to go to London tomorrow. You'll be in charge of K Section for a week. Take it easy. Sidonie will hold down your desk for you at Twenty Annapolis. Whatever synthesizing has to be done, she'll do it. Holcomb will run the rest of the office and attend the weekly briefings with State, and tomorrow's briefings with Joint Chiefs. That gives you some free time for Bela Korvuth."

"You said over the phone he left word with some farmer that he was going to gun for me."

"Yes. Does it worry you?"

Durell smiled. "I'd be a fool if it didn't. But it's not quite the way you think."

"No? Well, I'm taking it seriously, too. I'm going to put a couple of men to watch Deirdre. She won't know they're around, but we don't want anything happening to her, and a man like Bela Korvuth may decide to hit you from any direction. There's your grandfather, too, down in Bayou Peche Rouge. Not much chance of Korvuth getting down there, but you never can tell. There's no point in guessing how much they know about you in the AVO and MGB offices. Not since the Stella Marni case, anyway. We've got to assume they know as much about you in their dossiers as we've got on Bela Korvuth, which may even the odds a bit. I don't know. We'll have to play it by ear."

"One thing I don't understand," Durell said. "Korvuth is a professional. He's been in the game longer than I. This whole thing is too easy. He didn't have to come over here disguised as a Hungarian refugee. A dozen other ways would have been better for him. And nobody in the business would deliberately break his own cover by talking to a local farmer about his mission. It doesn't make sense."

McFee sighed and nodded and looked out through the small window of the shelter hut toward the waiting plane. He somehow managed to fill the small room with his presence and the quiet strength of his personality. Durell often wondered about this small gray man who knew so much, whose connections made a web that girdled the world, and whose job was the anonymous direction of strategy in this dark, silent war that seemed to go on forever.

"I was wondering how soon it would occur to you, Sam," he said. "You're going to have to be very careful."

"Is Korvuth a blind, then?"

"We don't know. Your guess at this stage of the game is as good as mine. You've seen his picture?" When Durell shook his head, McFee took out a small leather folder containing a photograph of a gray-haired man of about forty, with mild eyes and a saddle nose and a prim little bowtie. "Don't let him see you first, Sam. Looks like a small-time business man, doesn't he? Looks harmless, eh?"

"No, not harmless," Durell said. He had felt a quick twist of something turning over in him when McFee suggested a guard for Deirdre. He wasn't sure, but it could have been fear for her, and this dismayed him, because he knew he should not be thinking of anything now except the job McFee was discussing. He knew McFee was watching him, an objective curiosity in the little general's pale gray eyes. He didn't think anything showed in his face as he went on. "The eyes in this photo are all wrong. It shows there, and in his mouth, too. Is Korvuth a Magyar?"

"Hard to tell about these people. I pulled what we had on friend Bela out of the dossier files, but it isn't much. The rest of the physical description makes him about five-ten, weight one-seventy, a little paunchy, but awfully, awfully fast. So don't let his sloppy physique fool you. It isn't that way at all. His hair is brown, his eyes are brown, and he's got a steel-capped molar in the lower right jaw. We got that from a dentist in Buda who worked on Korvuth last year."

"All right," Durell said. "Don't kid me about it, please."

"I'm not kidding. There's nothing to laugh about or ignore about this man. Bela Korvuth is probably the greatest master of political assassination and sudden death since the Middle Ages. We know he was responsible for the disappearance of Boganov in Prague two years ago, when Boganov anticipated the swing away from Stalin and jumped the gun. Now the pendulum is reversed, and even if they had let Boganov live, he'd be in the doghouse again. Then there was the poisoning of Imre Kardovi in Bucharest last year, the death of the wife of a Soviet attache in London six months ago—she had fallen in love with a junior clerk in Downing Street—and there was the killing of those two MGB boys who made contact with Frank Duggan in Rome and wanted to peddle a few secrets to us. You can check the rest of it in the office when you get a chance. But you have to get an idea of what this man is, Sam. When the freedom fighters in Hungary were stringing up AVO men by the heels from lampposts in Budapest, Korvuth was giving orders to machine-gun women and children in Parliament Square, and we know he personally organized the deportation movement when the Russians sent in their Mongolian troops. Another idea of what sort of man this is, and his nerve, is the fact that he deliberately took the chance of mingling with the refugees to get over here, when he'd have been torn to pieces by them if they learned who he was. All I want to impress on you is that this man is as good or better than you. I don't want to lose you on this, Sam. And he's here to do a double job."

"It still doesn't add up," Durell said, frowning.

"Well, he was Stella Marni's lover back in Budapest in fifty-four. We just got that recently. You put the Marni woman on ice six months ago, and he's going to enjoy cutting your heart out."

"No," Durell said, "he's too professional to let that bother him." He lit a cigarette, to McFee's annoyance. It was close and hot in the shelter hut, with a kerosene stove going full blast. McFee didn't smoke. "Any guesses on the other victim he's going after?"

"We can't afford to guess. It's up to you to find out."

"What about this Zoltan Ske? And the woman?"

"We don't have anything useful on either of them, Sam. Just the cover stories they used at our Vienna office to get flown over here with the last group of Hungarian refugees. You can get their pictures from Breagan."

"Check," Durell said. "Now what do you really think, general?"

"I agree with you. It's all a blind."

"You believe they'd throw away a man like Bela Korvuth just to keep us busy while they try for another objective?"

"Yes. I see it that way, Sam."

"Would Korvuth know it?" Then Durell could have bitten his tongue. "Sorry. Of course, Korvuth has to know he's the patsy. I must be a little tired. Korvuth would never break his cover this way, otherwise. For him, it might well be a suicide mission; and he's got to know that. He'd obey orders, of course."

McFee looked uncertain. "Maybe I'd better put Holcomb on this, Sam. You may be too close to it—what with Deirdre, and all. But I don't see how you can stay out of it, anyway, with Korvuth after you."

"I'll be all right," Durell said. "What do you think Bela Korvuth is trying to cover with his sacrifice?"

McFee said irritably: "Put out that damned cigarette, will you, Sam? It's the refugees, of course. We've heard rumors about a number of their agents getting through on innocent covers. Maybe a dozen, in all. We've got to know who they are and where they are—every last one of them. It's probably a highly specialized sabotage crew, ready to take up jobs and ordinary lives and officially vanish—but with the difference that these dozen or more people are going to be dedicated to the proposition that when a certain day comes, they can and must and will paralyze something vital to our national defense. We're supposed to forget about that possibility while we chase after Korvuth and try to stop him from getting his announced victims—you, and Mr. X, whoever the poor devil may be. It's damned clever of them, really. We can't afford to ignore Korvuth's being here. We've got to find him and stop him. There's nothing small or unimportant about his mission here, and that's what makes it even more important to find out what he's been sent to cover up. A sort of double-threat play, as I see it. The old one-two. It's going to have to work out fast, before our dedicated friends get too well set in their cover personalities and too deep in the ground for us to dig them out in time."

"You think it may begin with Korvuth?" Durell asked.

"Bela Korvuth's aim is to lead us away from the infiltration of the crew that came in with the innocent refugees. He'll certainly try to lead us down the primrose path into a blind alley. The sooner he's stopped, the better. At the same time, Korvuth might possibly be a connecting link to the other apparatus. We can't tell. It's up to you to find out, Sam."

"Then I'd better get up there."

"You'll work with Breagan in Jersey," McFee said. "As long as the trail stays there, anyway. After that, you're on your own. Call for help at Twenty Annapolis, if you need any. Holcomb will assist, if I'm not back from Europe yet. Try to keep your cover intact, Sam. We don't know how much Korvuth really knows about you, but we've got to assume the worst and hope for the best, understand?"

Durell nodded. He was suddenly impatient to be going. McFee had nothing more for him. He looked at his watch. It was almost eleven o'clock in the morning.

Chapter Three

AT TWELVE-THIRTY Durell met Matt Breagan in the kitchen of the Dunstermeir farm in New Jersey. Almost six hours had gone by since Bela Korvuth, Zoltan Ske and the woman known as Ilona had made their break from the refugee reception center at Kilmer. The perimeter of the search area had narrowed considerably, with no tangible results. A sense of discouragement and futility was plainly stamped on Breagan's square, tired face.

It was still snowing, and Durell was grateful for the tweed overcoat he had worn. He stood in the center of the shining, clean kitchen, his feet slightly apart. The Dunstermeirs, man and wife, stood in an attitude of patient waiting; their faces were like rock, expressionless, betraying no particular interest in Durell, who was not introduced by name.

Breagan said, "So far, we haven't spotted the truck or the hired hand, Endre, who drove off with Korvuth and his crew. It's been snowing steadily, and by the time we got here, the tracks of the truck were pretty well covered. They seemed to turn out to the road, wich had been plowed just a few minutes before that time, and they were lost there."

"I'll have a look later," Durell said. "Right now I'm more interested in the hired hand. Endre Stryzyk, that's his name?"

"Yes," Dunstermeir said.

"How long have you had him with you?"

"Over six months now. We took him from Kilmer. A fine boy. We had no suspicions of him at all."

"Do you mean he went with this man willingly?"

"Endre seemed to know the man. It was almost as if he had been waiting for him." Dunstermeir turned his thin gray head toward his wife as she made a small, almost unaudible sound. The woman abruptly turned away toward the big iron and nickel stove. "Naturally, we had no suspicions," the farmer went on. "You people are supposed to check the ones coming in now, not so? We accepted the fact that it was safe to employ him."

"And you don't think so now?" Durell asked.

Dunstermeir only shrugged.

"What was your occupation in Germany before you came here?" Durell asked suddenly.

The man's mouth twitched. "I was—I was also a farmer."

"You don't speak like one. Where did you learn English?"

"Am I under suspicion, too?"

"It is not impossible. Answer the question, please."

"I went to the University of Bonn. But I left Germany long before the war. Our two sons were forced to stay over there. They were killed in Normandy, finally."

"You should have suggested they were killed on the Eastern front, fighting Russians," Durell said coldly.

"But they were not killed there. The English killed them."

"And you were not a farmer then," Durell stated flatly.

"No. No, I was an engineer. Here, one does what one can."

"And what was Endre's occupation before coming over?"

"He was not one for speaking much about himself. He was young, you understand. About twenty-two or -three. One of the young freedom fighters, he claimed. He said he had no family, no occupation, except for having had odd jobs here and there in Budapest. But he was a hard worker."

"You speak of him as if he's gone for good."

"We will not employ him again, if he comes back."

"Because he seemed to know Korvuth?"

"Yes. Endre knew him."

"And he drove the truck willingly?"

"Let us say that he seemed to be resigned to it."

"I'd like to look at the place where you kept the truck," Durell said.

Dunstermeir shrugged. "This side of the dairy barn."

Durell went out with Breagan. Breagan didn't have much to say as they walked into the cutting sleet that slanted across the dooryard toward the big red barn. Beyond the immediate environs of farmhouse and outbuildings, the land reached in flat fields for half a mile toward a line of woods, black against the lowering gray sky. The coating of ice and snow had been thoroughly trampled by troopers' feet and rutted by the police cars that had come and gone throughout the morning. Durell kept his annoyance about this to himself.

There were about thirty Guernseys and a dozen Swiss Browns in the cattle stalls inside the barn. Durell looked for modern milking machines, but there were few of the conveniences and mechanical equipment used by most farmers. He stood in the warm, moist atmosphere of the barn, hearing the restless movements of the cows, checking with quick glances the equipment, the loft, the bales of hay towering high against the barn walls.

"What bothers you, Breagan?" he asked quietly.

"The same thing that troubles you, Sam. Dunstermeir was an engineer. Engineers believe in the efficiency of machinery."

"Maybe he's having a hard time financially."

"Not in this day of credit and time payments," Breagan said.

Durell nodded. "What is he covering for?"

"Bela Korvuth. Maybe others. Shall I pull him in?"

"Not yet." Durell frowned. "As long as we've got a peek at one cog of their apparatus, we know it's there and we can handle it when we find it necessary. No use smashing it until we see where it leads. But it's a start."

"Do you think Korvuth is still around?"

"No. But Endre ought to be."

He walked through a doorway in a partition of the barn that led to a garage area and workshop. Two tractors stood here, on a concrete apron, and a 1949 Chevrolet sedan, probably Dunstermeir's personal car. It was clean and polished, betraying the man's innate efficiency. There was space for another vehicle, probably the missing stake-body truck. Durell lifted the wide overhead door and stepped outside, scanning the glitter of snow that covered the fields to his right. Faint imprints of tires, not completely filled in yet by the wind-driven sleet, curved away in both directions from the apron.

"Dunstermeir is watching from an upstairs window," Breagan said.

"I know."

"Why do you think Endre is still around?"

Durell didn't answer at once. He kept studying the tire prints—not those that led to the nearby highway, but the twin traces that curved away over the fields toward the woods.

"If Dunstermeir is part of Korvuth's apparatus," he said, "then Endre is not. Otherwise, Dunstermeir wouldn't have tried to make us suspicious of Endre. That means the boy is on our side. He recognized Korvuth as a bigwig in the AVH, tried to break for it, and had to be taken along. We're probably much too late to help him, Matt."

Breagan looked troubled. "I should have thought of it."

"Let's get your car," Durell said.

They drove away from the farmhouse, across the open field toward the woods. In places, the wind and sleet had obliterated all traces of the tire marks Durell followed. A wire fence helped guide him toward the distant woods, and as they drew nearer, a small barway became visible and a narrow lane opened, cutting through the maples and oaks that creaked under the weight of ice and snow. Here the tracks were more distinct, clearly those of a truck. There was a small wooden bridge over a frozen stream, a curve to the right, and they had found their objective.

The truck stood in a small clearing, surrounded by scraggly cedars that cut it off from view of the farm and the highway. Durell got out and looked around. Other cars had been here—two, maybe three—and recently, since the snow had begun falling this morning. Breagan began to curse in a monotone.

"They've got away."

Durell nodded. "Yes. And separately."

The lane they had followed kept going through the woods, probably to a secondary dirt road that in turn would open into the highway to New Brunswick. Their quarry had long since escaped the net that hundreds of men had been trying to draw tight since dawn.

"I'd better pull Dunstermeir in," Breagan said.

"No. Let him roam free for a day or two. He might lead us to something. I'm worried about this Endre Stryzyk, though."

Durell walked back toward the wooden bridge. Breagan followed, moving stiffly with the cold. His lips were blue. Durell paid no attention to the icy wind as he climbed down the embankment and peered for a long time under the bridge where it crossed the frozen, ice-bound stream.

"Here he is. The poor devil."

The body of a straw-haired young man lay huddled between the western piers of the bridge, crammed against the hard earthen embankment among stiff and brittle weeds. One foot had broken the ice in the stream and lay in the black, running water. It was a clumsy killing, and Durell wondered about it. No real attempt had been made to hide the body from even this cursory search. It was almost as if Bela Korvuth wanted his victim found, perhaps as a warning to other freedom fighters who had come here for refuge, perhaps as a cover for his true assignment. The man was certainly not behaving as a carefully trained agent should; but this, according to McFee, was precisely the way he was supposed to act. Durell didn't like it. He knew the way the Moscow school operated, and he could anticipate and counter the moves of their men almost by rote; but this was like operating against an erratic amateur whose blunders could not be anticipated and whose extravagantly careless moves could cause a backfire equally disastrous to himself. Uneasiness touched him for a moment and he straightened quickly, his eyes scanning the bleak wilderness of cedar woods and pin oaks. The wind made the brittle branches rattle overhead. Visibility was not very good in any direction. The sleet stung his face, narrowed his eyes. There was nothing to see. Bela Korvuth wasn't here.

Endre had been killed by a single bow that had broken his neck. His young face told Durell nothing. There was a pathetic, lonely quality about this ending, the way he had been abandoned here, carelessly and heartlessly, in this freezing dark space under an alien bridge. It was a long way from the street fighting in Budapest, a sad ending to the enthusiastic fighting this youth had engaged in for freedom. Durell knew it had not been necessary to kill the boy, even though Endre had undoubtedly recognized Korvuth from the AVH in Budapest. But maybe the boy had overheard Korvuth talking to Dunstermeir in a way that meant his elimination was necessary. Durell could not be sure of this, and he didn't waste time in further speculation. Breagan could take care of the details necessary to cleaning up here.

The trail at this spot was as cold as the dead man's body.

Chapter Four

DURELL had lunch in Trenton with Matt Breagan, and then boarded a train for New York. It was two o'clock when he sat waiting in a small, barren room, sparsely furnished, not far from Foley Square. He waited alone. There were only a desk, two oak chairs, and a long, battered library table pushed against the wall opposite the desk. The windows were covered with black shades, and the single light in the ceiling shed a garish blaze over the dull yellow walls. A steam radiator hissed and sputtered under the windows, and Durell stood near it, tall and dark, his eyes troubled.

It had been necessary to make these arrangements because of Bela Korvuth. He did not want anyone in the New York office to know he was here, or what he was doing, because it was possible that Korvuth might anticipate this move.

At ten minutes after two a guard brought in Stella Marni.

The guard nodded to Durell, looked at Stella Marni, and closed the door to wait outside. Stella stood where she was, just one step inside the bleak little room.

"So it is you," she said quietly.

"Hello, Stella."

"I would rather not be here."

"I'm sorry. It's necessary."

"I have nothing to say to you."

"Perhaps you do. Please sit down, Stella."

He was shocked by the change in her, but he looked merely polite and solicitous as she seated herself. She wore a simple gray dress, and her long blonde hair had been cropped by the prison matron. There was only a touch of lipstick on her mouth. She wore no belt with her dress, and her shoes were simple, soft slippers with no metal on them at all. She had tried to kill herself a week after Durell had brought about her imprisonment, and since then she had been watched carefully.

She had been the most beautiful woman Durell had ever known, and she had caused him to come perilously close to losing his life and everything dear to him, because of what she was, and because he believed she had loved him, in those days so many months ago, when he was tracing her down as the head of a coercion ring working to force refugees to go back behind the Iron Curtain. He did not underestimate her. She was brilliant and heartless, certainly a murderess, and one of the most devastating operators Durell had ever worked against. He respected her. Seeing her now, her face pale, her beauty faded by the months in prison, he still felt a quick little twist inside him, remembering a night they had spent together, making love, at a time when he had believed in her innocence and would have fought anything and anyone for her.

She knew what he was thinking, and her smile was wry. "It is all over now, Sam, is it not?"

"Yes. The old part of it. You and I both made our share of mistakes, Stella."

"No one is perfect, not even in our profession. We can never be friends again, can we? We were once lovers, but never friends. And you won, after all."

"Please sit down," he said.

"Why are you here?"

"Are you well?" he asked. "Are you being treated all right?"

She smiled. "Please. Of course."

For one moment she lifted her gaze and he remembered the way her pale green eyes had moved him, long ago, the way he had wondered at the ivy façade of this once-beautiful woman. She had been a statue carved of cold marble that for a few hours, alone with him, had melted into a desperate and passionate woman. He forced himself to dismiss the images in his memory. He saw that she still smiled secretively as she sat down, folding her hands placidly in her lap. Her blonde hair had lost some of its luster and looked dull now. He wondered how old she really was. She looked older than he had remembered. Older, and defeated.

"I'm here because I need some help," he began quietly.

"Not from me. Your people have questioned me many times, as you probably know. I'll never discuss anything with you. I do not want your pity, your favors, or your love. Some day we will win, and I will be set free. Then, perhaps, we will meet again. If you are still alive, Sam. I do not think you will be. A man in your job is not a good insurance risk, as they say. You have already lived past your time. It will not be long now. You look tired. One day you will make a slip, just one little error, and then it will all be over."

"Do you wish that for me?"

"I don't think about you any more."

"Your day may be a long time coming."

"I have patience," she said.

He lit a cigarette and handed it to her, careful not to let their fingers touch. She crossed her legs, tugged at the simple gray prison dress. She had lost weight, he noticed, and her cheeks were hollow and shadowed. Again, when she lifted her glance to meet his, he felt the impact of her enormous jade eyes. She smiled.

"What sort of help do you need, Sam?"

"It's about Bela Korvuth," he said bluntly. "I want to know all about him. Everything you can tell me. I won't make any promises to you, Stella, you know better than that, but it could be easier for you to wait and be patient, if you helped me now. I could see to that."

"Bela?" she repeated.

"He was your friend in Budapest, wasn't he?"

"My lover, you mean. If you know he was my friend, you know we shared an apartment for two years." She smiled again, and he did not like it. "Yes, Bela was my lover. It was some years ago. It was not a good thing, really, considering that we each had our jobs to do, without thought for a personal life. And I was so ambitious. But what we had then, was good."

"But you were never really in love with him?"

She looked up suddenly. "Are you going to tell me that Bela is dead?"

"No, he isn't. He's here, in this country."

She stood up. She was agitated, he could see, and he was relieved that his guess about a direct, blunt approach was working to this extent. He watched her walk, and the fine coordination of her magnificent body was exactly the same as he remembered it. He wished he didn't think so often of the past, when he was with her.

"You don't have him in custody, however, or you wouldn't be here," she pointed out.

"That's true."

"And you want him very badly."

"That's also true."

"Not from me," she said. "Never from me."

"Sit down, Stella. I haven't finished. Bela came in with the last group of refugees from your home town of Budapest. He broke out before he could be picked up and he left with a man named Zoltan Ske and a woman, Ilona, who posed as his wife." He waited, but nothing changed in her face. "We're pretty anxious to haul in all three of them."

"Ilona?" she asked curiously.

"Posing as his wife," he repeated.

"Do you imagine this makes me jealous?"

He grinned. He looked different for a moment. "I rather hoped it might."

"You should know better than that. We cannot allow our private emotions to interfere with the work we must do. Surely you, who are one of the best, know all about that."

"Doesn't it bother you at all that he's with another woman?"

She looked defiant and proud. "Why should it? I slept with you, did I not? Did it trouble you, then?"

"Stella—"

Now she was angry. "Why is Bela here? Do you know that?"

"He has announced that he's going to kill me," Durell said quietly.

She stared at him. Her pale lips were slightly parted. Then she shook her head stubbornly. "No, no. He would never do such a foolish thing. He is not an amateur. He would not give you warning first."

"Well, he did. I guess you can understand why. It's a ruse, of course, to throw us off balance while something else is accomplished."

"So?"

"Which doesn't mean he'll ignore me. He'll still try to kill me, all right."

"Then you should be frightened, Sam," she said softly. She was smiling again. "Bela is an expert at that sort of thing. He will succeed, you know. He has never failed yet. You are as good as dead, standing here right now, at this moment." Her green eyes were searching, cool and objective. "But you never showed fear when I knew you. Can you be afraid now? Is this why you came to me, so I might help you to save yourself?"

"I want to find Bela before he gets someone else."

"He has another target?"

"Of course," Durell said. "I'm only secondary. Third-string objective, really. We're pretty sure he's covering for a bigger, entirely different operation, that concerns your countrymen and the freedom fighters who've taken sanctuary over here. Bela is trying to keep us off balance by looking for him while the real operation gets set."

"Ah, you're always so damned clever," she whispered bitterly.

"Surely there's something you know that can help us," Durell insisted. "You could do yourself some good by co-operating."

Stella Marni was silent. In the harsh glare of the single light in the barren room, she looked older and more drawn than before. Yet she was still one of the most beautiful women Durell had ever known. There was a sleek grace to the articulation of her body as she rose with her hands clasped before her.

She paced briefly back and forth across the little room. It was a good sign, Durell thought, all this agitation. Six months ago she would never have yielded to it. He tried to consider her objectively, forcing away all memories of past intimacies. He crushed out his cigarette in a glass ashtray on the desk and stood waiting until Stella Marni turned and looked at him.

There was nothing but hatred in her eyes.

"I hope Bela kills you," she whispered. "I hope he lets you know it is he, before he does it. And then you will know that it is being done for me, and for no other reason, just before you die."

Durell sighed. "I had hoped you were changed."

"You should have known better than that."

"I suppose, in reality, I did." There was nothing to be gained here, he decided. It had only been an off-chance, at best. He rang a bell on the desk for the guard, and Stella stood watching him, calm and lovely and wishing him dead, and nothing moved in her face.

When he left, he knew he would never see her again.

Chapter Five

HE WAS being followed. Durell spotted the girl as soon as he left the building. The work was done clumsily, although he would have recognized a shadowing job even if it had been done by the most expert tail in the business. For a few minutes, during the taxi ride back to Pennsylvania Station, he wondered if Dickinson McFee had assigned someone to keep an eye on him and cover his back. But nobody in K Section would have been so obvious. Nor would McFee have put a girl to trail him his way.

She wore a red felt hat, which was a mistake, of course, and a belted cloth coat and red rubber boots against the sleet and slush that covered the city streets. He saw her when he hailed his cab, and knew that she had gotten into one that had been waiting for her. When he arrived at the terminal, she was only a few moments behind him. He could have lost her then quite easily in the crowded station, but he did not want to do that. Neither did he want to double back just yet and take her before he learned how far she was ready to go.

She got on the Washington-bound train with him.

It could be, he thought, that his move to see Stella Marni had been anticipated, and he was alert for danger, his reflexes primed for quick action. But nothing happened. The girl in the red hat took a seat about a third of the way behind him in the coach, on the aisle, and apparently became absorbed in her newspaper. Durell made no move to get a closer look at her just then. It would have been too obvious; she might have been alerted to his awareness of her, and perhaps frightened off. Yet he had a fair idea of her appearance, a hint of dark coppery hair tucked under the absurd red hat, crisp curls dampened by the snow, long legs under a primly conservative woolen skirt. Her face was pleasant, with prominent cheek-bones, not striking or unusual, except for her large eyes that seemed to be dark brown, or perhaps black; he couldn't be sure.

There was a delay of about ten minutes at North Philadelphia Station, and Durell got off the train to find a public telephone booth on the platform. It was growing dark now. He put through a call to Deirdre Padgett in Prince John, Maryland.

The telephone rang three or four times and Durell heard a click and then it rang again.

"Art?" he said.

There was silence.

"Come on, Art, this is Sam. Are you bugging Dee's line?"

"Oh. Hi, Cajun." It was Art Greenwald, the electronics expert of K Section. There was nothing Art couldn't do with wiretaps and recordings. "Wish you were back in the bayous in this weather, Sam?"

"Where is Deirdre?" he asked.

"Around somewhere, I reckon."

"Why doesn't she answer?"

"Search me. The little Napoleon told me to tap all calls. What goes on?"

"Who's watching her house?"

"Lew Franklin and George Mester. I'm at a little place up the shore. Good place for ducks. She's still at home, Sam. Don't worry about it."

"Let it ring some more, then," Durell said.

He listened to the repetitive, mechanical sounds in the receiver. A strange urgency began to work in him. Through the glass of the telephone booth, he saw the girl in the red hat step off the train and look anxiously up and down the wet platform. She looked worried, and then she looked directly at him in the booth and turned away, a bit too quickly, betraying herself. She walked past the booth to the newsstand nearby.

Deirdre did not answer the phone.

"Art," Durell said. "Send George and Low to look in on her."

"Maybe she's just gone for a little walk," Greenwald suggested.

"I'd like to check on it."

"Right, Cajun." Greenwald paused. "One thing. If you want to see our little Napoleon before he leaves for London, meet him at the airport. Where in hell are you, anyway?"

"Philadelphia."

"He's taking off at eight. Can you make it?"

"I'll make it. Let him know. And check Deirdre, will you?"

"Over and out," Greenwald said lightly.

Durell hung up. His uneasiness and urgency did not leave him. When he got back on the train, the girl in the red hat was already in her seat.

He wanted to go straight to Prince John, but there wasn't time for that. He reached the National Airport half an hour before flight time, and the girl in the red hat was still behind him—a little clumsier now, with darkness complicating her problem. Durell deliberately made it easier for her. He did not want to lose her any more than she seemed to want to lose him. Yet he could not allow her to see him make contact with Dickinson McFee.

It was raining in Washington, with a raw northerly wind whipping the huge airport. The waiting room was only moderately crowded. No flights had been cancelled, and Durell walked through, knowing the girl was still behind him, until he saw Dickinson McFee standing alone near one of the ticket booths. He did not stop or change his stride in any way, but as he went by the small gray man, he moved the fingers of his left hand in a signal that meant McFee was to follow. Durell went into one of the men's rooms and washed his hands, smoked a cigarette, and wondered what the girl in the red hat would do now. He had to wait eight minutes before McFee showed.

The little gray man washed his hands at the next basin beside Durell. They did not look at each other, and McFee's mouth did not move when he spoke under and through the mechanical sound of the speakers from the announcer's booth.

"The one in the red hat?" he said.

"She picked me up in New York," Durell told him. "I went to see Stella Marni. Nothing doing there. She wishes me dead."

"And they anticipated the move?"

"I sort of hoped Bela Korvuth would be there waiting for a try at me. No such luck. He sent the girl, instead. I gather she's the one we know as Ilona."

"Right. You've got a thread in your hand, with her."

"But she's working alone," Durell said. "Nobody is on the tail with her. I've checked and double-checked."

"So did I," McFee said. "In the waiting room. Has she used a telephone yet?"

"Not unless she's on one now, contacting Korvuth."

"Do you want her picked up?"

Durell reached for the roll of paper toweling and dried his hands. Several men had entered the washroom, and he could see them in the mirror before him, and the way he kept his hands was such that he could move either one instantly. For just a moment he met McFee's gray eyes in the mirror.

"Looks clean. I don't want the girl touched yet," Durell said. "As you suggest, she's a thread, and I don't want to snap it too soon. It's a piece of luck, perhaps. Korvuth got clean away in New Jersey, with Zoltan Ske. He killed Dunstermeir's hired hand—a boy named Endre Stryzyk. The kid may have spotted him as top brass in Budapest's AVH."

"I heard about it," McFee said. "We've got something working on the other track, too. The operation Korvuth is trying to smoke-screen. It figures that every one of the cells we suspect got in with the innocent Hungarians must speak perfect, idiomatic English, must be absolutely Americanized to speed their assimilation and disappearance into the populace. It's quite a list, and maybe most of them covered what they know about the language. But Hungerford is checking that out, along with the FBI people. It will be a long job— a good many of those folks have scattered to new homes and jobs all over the country by now. There's nothing you can do on that until you get the list. Even then, it will be a routine check job. Unless, of course, you manage to get the names somehow out of Korvuth. Bela might know, what with his background in the secret police, and all that. But he's smart and tricky." McFee dried his hands, too. "I can't figure the girl tagging you, can you?"

"She hasn't been well trained. She's pretty clumsy."

"That's what doesn't check out," McFee agreed.

"I'll talk to her before the night is over. Anything else on Korvuth's other quarry, aside from me?"

"Call the office on it. We've doubled security on all the top men in nuclear, rocket, and satellite work. But Korvuth is shifty. We may not know who he's after, aside from you, until it's too late. Pentagon is raising hell with us now, crying wolf for their egghead sheep. But you can't watch these scientific people too closely; they're temperamental. They don't want to be coddled or swathed in cotton wool. And it takes more men than our budget allows to do the job right."

"It will be easier to nail Korvuth before he begins executing," Durell suggested. "Maybe our Ilona can help."

"Use your own judgment. I'm off for London now. Anything else I can do?"

"I'm a little troubled about Deirdre. She doesn't answer her phone in Prince John. Do you have anything on that?"

McFee made a negative signal. "I wouldn't go near her, if I were you. Not with this girl on your tail. Good luck, Sam."

The little man turned away from the wash basin and was gone. Durell went into one of the booths to wait a few minutes before following him out into the main waiting room. McFee had vanished.

The girl in the red hat was gone, too.

He used the telephone booth at the airport to call Deirdre again. Uneasiness still roweled him. And again the phone rang without reply until he heard Art Greenwald's wiretap click softly.

"Art? Sam, again. What goes on?"

Greenwald sounded a little worried. "She's there, Sam. The house is lighted, and Franklin can see her walking around inside. He went in to talk to her after you called before. He had to tell her a little of what's happening. But everything seemed okay."

"Then why doesn't she answer the phone?"

"You've got me there, Cajun."

Durell touched his small, dark mustache with a fingertip. From the booth, he could see most of the waiting room, and the girl known as Ilona had not reappeared. He wondered if he had dangerously underestimated her clumsiness. It could have been a smart subterfuge to make him careless about contacting McFee. Maybe she had followed him just to be led to McFee. His worry increased. But then she couldn't have boarded the plane with the chief. She had to be somewhere in the near vicinity.

"Sam?"

"I think I'd better come over, Art."

"I'll let the boys know."

"All right. But keep them away from the house now. I don't want to contact them when I arrive."

"You think something is wrong?"

"Very wrong," Durell said, and hung up.

His car, a dark-blue Buick coupe, had been taken back by McFee from the Prince John airport earlier this morning and parked in front of his apartment house. Durell took a cab to retrieve it. Nobody was waiting in ambush here, and he lifted the hood to inspect the engine briefly. It was still raining, and the night was dark and cold. He drove quickly and expertly through Washington's traffic, found the small asphalt road that twisted through black countryside eastward, and arrived in Prince John at nine o'clock.

Deirdre's house, on the Chesapeake shore, was at the end of a long lane that twisted through wooded countryside, following the water's edge. He drove to within a quarter of a mile of the place and parked the car near a fenced pasture. The rain felt like a spray of ice against his face, and he turned up the collar of his coat against the wind, checking the weight of his snubby .38 in the under-arm holster of his conservative blue suit. From where he left his car he could see a gleam of light through the thrashing traceries of the trees, and as he moved farther along the lane toward the beach, he saw it was the riding light of old Tom Yordie's pungy. He moved on like a shadow, soundless amid the restless crackling of small branches in the wind and the hiss and patter of cold rain on the carpet of dead oak leaves underfoot.

He was sure now that something was very wrong here.

Through the rain he heard the muted pulsing of the pungy's old motor as the craft anchored in the cove. The gatekeeper's cottage was dark and empty as he approached, and a shadow that was now only a shadow moved ever so slightly in the doorway, revealing a fleeting glimpse of a man's angular face. Lew Franklin. Franklin had not seen him. Durell went by, close enough to hear Franklin sigh in discomfort in the rain.

The main house was an old Georgian structure of faded rose brick, with twin chimneys and a wide lawn and a once-famous rose garden. Deirdre was the last of the Maryland Padgetts, and she used this place only on weekends from her fashion editor's job in Washington. Lights shone yellow from the library windows facing the Chesapeake, and another light shone from the Dutch door to the kitchen in the north wing, facing the oyster-shell driveway. Durell saw no movement inside. He waited and watched and waited again.

There was nothing to see or hear. Only the rain, and the idling mutter of the pungy's engine in the cove two hundred yards beyond the gentle swoop of the beach. Durell paused under a dripping old giant of a sycamore tree.

He could almost smell the trap closing in around him.

It added up. Deirdre had no reason to refuse to answer the phone. The fact that Franklin had gone in to talk to her meant nothing. Lew didn't know her, he couldn't have been sensitive to the fact that she might have been acting, with seeming naturalness, under duress. He was sure now that someone else was in the house with Deirdre. Someone who knew he would come back for her.

It had to be Bela Korvuth.

Long ago, as a boy in Bayou Peche Rouge, Durell had learned to weigh odds with the cool and calculating precision of a professional gambler. His old grandfather, Jonathan, had taught him every trick of the trade, gleaned from a lifetime spent as a gambler on the old Mississippi sidewheelers. Standing there, watching Deirdre's gracious house, Durell could see the old man now, straight and tall and white-maned, in the pilot house of the *Three Belles*, the old steamboat Jonathan had run into the bayou mudflats and used as his home. The old man had taught him carefully and patiently.

"There be all kinds of traps, Samuel, and the important thing is to learn how to use 'em, every one. First thing, know they're there. Then look it over real careful and figure how you can make it bite the trapper. If you can't do that, steer clear. If you can, then you win pot, table, and break the bank."

Durell watched the house. The thought that she was in danger, the knowledge intuitive in him that something was wrong here, with Deirdre being used as a lure to bring him to his death, kindled more than anger. He had an impulse to charge inside and get her safe and free. But he held everything in check, the fear and the anger together, waiting until the cool, analytical training imposed on his temperament gained the upper hand.

The house was quiet. The light shone with a steady yellow from the windows, bleaching the rain to silver. The pungy still idled in the nearby cove. He looked back for Franklin, did not see him. Franklin's partner was also invisible, and Durell guessed he was stationed at the boathouse on the shore side of the house. Nothing moved that he could see. Then he suddenly glimpsed Deirdre rise from a wing chair inside the library and move toward a table and take a cigarette. Her back was straight and stiff. She had changed her clothes and wore a flannel gray skirt and a dark red sweater that accented the sweeping raven wings of her hair. He could not see her face clearly, but there was enough in the way she moved to help confirm his estimate of the trap.

There were French doors in the north wing of the house, opening into the unused dining room. Durell moved silently toward them, trying the bronze lever handles very slowly, very gently. The doors were not locked. He left them as they were, being too inviting, and did not enter that way.

Another door, leading into what had been the servants' quarters in the same wing, was tightly closed. Durell worked at the lock with a small instrument he carried in a pocket of his wallet. In three minutes the door swung open and he stepped inside out of the rain.

This end of the house was closed off and unheated during the winter months, and the air felt cold and clammy, smelling of the salt-water tides in the Chesapeake. The darkness was like black velvet across his eyes. He knew his way, however, and eased down a short corridor that had windows opening to the marshes nearby and the scrub pines edging the cove. The riding light of the pungy winked through the rain; and then he was beyond the windows, at a stairway that led up to the servants' bedrooms. He reached the second floor this way and drifted toward the center of the house and the main staircase of the central hall. Light shone ahead of him, edging up from the lower floor. He was careful not to let his shadow slide along the wall ahead of him.

There was no sound at all from below.

He waited and listened.

Then he heard Deirdre say something indistinct, her words muffled by the library doors. A reply came—a man's voice, brief and sharp. Then silence. He seemed to hear the house breathing, sighing, waiting through the muted rattle of the icy rain outside. He moved down swiftly then, stood in the center hallway, aware of shadows all around him. His hands and whole body were integrated either for attack or defense.

Deirdre made a sudden muffled sound of pain.

Durell opened the library door, going in fast with the swing of the panel. Something moved in a blur beside him. He felt the jolt of the blow on his left forearm, saw Deirdre swinging to face him, the back of her hand to her mouth. Terror shone in her eyes. He saw the second man behind her and the glint of the gun in his hand—and he knew they had been waiting for him exactly like this, aware of his rejection of the open dining-room doors, thinking one step ahead of him all the way—until this moment.

Both men were good at their business. It was Bela Korvuth who stood behind Deirdre—a small, meek-looking man except for his eyes and his smile, this killer from the Hungarian AVH. The second one, Zoltan Ske, stepped from behind the door. His face was nervous, thin and horselike, with disheveled straw hair. The gun in his hand prodded at Durell. His English was perfect, even to a faint New York accent.

"You will be so good as to stand quite still, friend."

Korvuth nodded and said, "We've been waiting for you, Mr. Durell."

"I know that," Durell said. He looked at Deirdre. "Are you all right?"

"They've been here for hours," she whispered quickly. "Here, in this house. They're going to kill you, Sam."

He looked at Korvuth. "Can you tell me why?"

Korvuth's smile was cold and bleak. "Perhaps because of Stella, and what you did to her. Because it has been decided by higher echelons that you are too dangerous and should be eliminated to end your record against us. We know all about you, Mr. Durell. You have been on our list for some time."

"I'm flattered that they sent an expert like you. But you didn't come over here just for me."

"Naturally not. I have other errands to perform."

"But none are really the main objective, are they?"

Korvuth sighed. His gun was held steady in Deirdre's back. He looked like a small, shabby business man in an old overcoat and a battered felt hat of brown. His dark, knitted tie was slightly askew under a limp, stained collar. It was his eyes that kept Durell immobile. They were pale, as hard as agates, void of any depths. A killer's eyes, with a mind behind them that had gone beyond any ordinary humanity, the eyes of a man who measured all life in only cold, mathematical terms, empty of any saving emotion.

"You are intelligent," Korvuth said softly. "Naturally, you guess what my real mission is. You know that I do not matter. And neither do you, except that your elimination may be of some small help to us."

"Let the girl go," Durell said. "We can do our business outside."

"On the contrary. I am not that simple. I understand your Western, bourgeois impulses toward chivalry. While I threaten her, you will not make a move. I respect your abilities, Mr. Durell, and I know your medieval impulses. One of the great weaknesses of your culture, this sloppy sentimentality. Zoltan?"

The nervous blond man beside Durell nodded jerkily. "We have been here too long already."

The trap was ready to spring, to deliver its death blow. Durell breathed lightly and easily. He looked at Deirdre and suddenly remembered what they had discussed that morning, at that peaceful breakfast, in a time that seemed to belong to another life and world. She had wanted to work for McFee, and he had warned her that her safety could not take precedence over his job. Now she read what he was thinking; she saw it in his eyes. And before her growing dismay became evident to these two men, Durell did what had to be done.

Zoltan Ske was just a little too nervous and anxious. He stood too near to him. Durell's move was fast, accurate, deadly. His hand chopped down precisely for the nerves in Ske's wrist. The gun jumped from the man's paralyzed fingers, hit the floor, bounced along the rug. There came a muffled report from Korvuth's gun. He saw the expression of surprise in Korvuth's flat face, the disbelief that Durell would act with the gun in Deirdre's back. Korvuth had counted on an emotional factor in Durell, and not on the training that had crushed and eliminated it. And because Korvuth had been sure Durell would yield to his threat against Deirdre, the man was thrown off balance for a few decisive seconds.

Deirdre fell, crumpling to the floor. Durell struck once more at Ske, driving the blond man stumbling against the wall, and then he jumped for Korvuth. The man fired wildly. The bullet chunked plaster from the ceiling. And then Durell had him, just for a moment, feeling the wild strength and agility of the man under his paunchy, nondescript façade.

Korvuth's gun went off again. It was an accident—the man was not aiming and couldn't aim while Durell gripped him— yet it happened, and Durell felt the jolting smash of the slug high up in his arm. The force of it broke his grip and he spun away, his hand still clinging to Korvuth's gun. But the man was free now, turning to the window. Durell pulled himself up, stumbling over Deirdre, and saw Zoltan Ske move toward the window, shouting something. There was a different shout from outside. Franklin's voice. Korvuth spun away toward the front door, panting, while Durell raised the man's gun. There was defeat in the other's pale eyes, and a promise of terror in the future. He got through the door before Durell could fire. And Durell, his right arm numb, managed to switch the gun to his left hand. He followed, nausea moving up in him, feeling the warmth of blood running down his arm under the texture of his suit. Zoltan Ske was already outside. A shot cracked. Korvuth was behind his companion, out in the rain on the wide, black lawn.

Durell yelled a warning to Franklin, but it was George Mester who made the mistake, coming at a dead run from the boathouse on the beach where he had been stationed. For an instant, it looked to Durell as if the trap had been sprung, in old Jonathan's words, to bite the biter. Then Mester fired, aiming well, and Zoltan Ske plunged face down on the lawn. Durell tripped over him and fell on his wounded shoulder, and an incredible shock of pain exploded all through his right side. He lost the gun he had taken from Bela Korvuth. He heard Mester shouting, and forced himself up again.

Lew Franklin ran up. "Sam, for God's sake, how did you get in there?"

"Never mind," Durell gasped. "Go after Korvuth."

George Mester joined them, a chunky man with gray hair. "He's in the woods, over there."

"Then get after him."

Lew Franklin nudged Zoltan Ske with his toe. In the rain and the darkness, Franklin looked young and uncertain. "What about this one?"

"I'm afraid he's dead," Durell said. "Damn it, I wanted to question him."

"Jesus, I'm sorry, Sam," Mester said.

"It's all right."

Both men looked at him, sensing something in his voice that should not have been there. "They were in the house, with Miss Padgett? They had her boxed in?"

"They wanted me," Durell said. "Korvuth had a gun on her. He thought it would keep me from making the play."

"Oh, hell," Franklin said. "I heard a shot in there, but I didn't think you'd—"

"Korvuth shot her," Durell said flatly. "Go ahead, get him."

"What about you? You're bleeding—"

"It's my arm. Nothing to worry about."

He watched the two men turn and run back across the lawn to the black edge of the scrub pine woods that bordered the marshes and the cove to the north. His stomach squirmed. He thought he was going to be sick. His legs felt weak. He held his right arm tightly, above the wound, and wondered how bad it really was. When he turned to walk back toward the house, the dark night reeled around him, but it was no darker or more despairing than the blackness inside him. He did not look back at the shapeless lump of shadow that Zoltan Ske's body made on the frozen lawn.

The front door stood open, streaming yellow light on the wet, crystalline grass. Durell swallowed. There was a feeling of unreality to the light, a feverish red tinge to it, as he walked slowly back up the steps into the house. He did not want to go inside. It was as if a vast, iron door had clanged shut inside him, since that moment he had made his move with Korvuth's gun on Deirdre. He had sacrificed her for the job. There was no other excuse he could give. He could not think about this and remain sane. It was as if something had torn apart inside him and he walked as if balanced on a delicate razor's edge, an empty pit of remorse to one side, a dreary waste of the future on the other. But he moved ahead mechanically to do what had to be done, a man who was more like a machine than flesh and blood.

He stood looking in the doorway to the library for a long tormented moment. There was a taste of bitter acid in the back of his throat.

Deirdre had not moved from where she had fallen in a crumpled heap to the carpeted floor. A pool of blood had gathered under her body, as brilliant and red as the sweater she wore. He noted the way the curve of her hip and thigh was held under the skirt and he remembered the fine, miraculous integration of her skin and flesh and bone. There was nothing about her that he had not known. She was as much a part of him as the bloody, shaking fingers he raised from the edge of the door.

"Dee?"

Her face was upturned, like a pale, crushed flower. Her eyes were closed. She did not seem to be breathing.

Chapter Six

S AM DURELL walked into the room slowly and knelt beside
her. The wound was in her shoulder, below the collar
bone, and from the slow pumping of blood he knew a large
vein had been severed. He lifted her limp wrist and felt for
a pulse. There was a dim and faraway beat that felt thready
under his anxious fingers. She was still alive.

"Dee," he whispered, "Dee, forgive me. I had to do it."

A faint whisper of breath between her lips made him wonder if she had heard his anguished words. He was no longer
conscious of the pain from his own wound. He wriggled out
of his coat and folded it and lifted her head to rest upon it,
and then he took his handkerchief and made a rough bandage
over the bleeding bullet hole, ripping at her clothing to get
at it. Leaving her, he went to the telephone and dialed the
operator, knowing that Art Greenwald would be listening in.

"There's been an accident," he said tersely, and he gave
Deirdre Padgett's name. "Send a doctor and an ambulance at
once."

When the operator rang off, Durell held the line open for
a moment, and Greenwald said: "Sam? You all right?"

"It's Deirdre. Korvuth was here."

"Damn it, how could—"

"We need some men, fast," Durell said. "He's in the woods
nearby. Zoltan Ske is dead. No sign of the girl. And Korvuth
got away."

He hung up and went back to Deirdre. As he knelt beside
her again he saw that her eyes were open and watching him
steadily, and he felt a vast wave of relief and thankfulness
wash over him, leaving him shaken and uncertain. "Dee, can
you hear me?"

"Yes, Sam," she whispered.

"You're going to be all right. I've sent for a doctor."

"Yes, I heard you." Her voice, her eyes were remote.
"Thank you."

"I'm sorry, Dee. So sorry."

She turned her head away from him. Her mouth shook and
he thought for a moment she was crying, but he couldn't be

sure. He looked down at the blood on his hand from his own wound, conscious of a dull throb of pain now.

"I had to do it. You understand that, don't you?"

"Did you get—did you kill him?"

"No. He got away."

She turned her head suddenly to look at him. Her eyes were cold, bright, incredibly angry. "Then you're wasting time, aren't you? Why bother to help me? You want to get out there and hunt him down, don't you? Don't waste any sympathy on me. You don't have to pretend anything. You've called for a doctor, and now you can go and do what you really want to do. Hunt and kill. It doesn't matter who else gets hurt, does it? I don't matter, and you don't count yourself as of any value to anyone, either, do you? Certainly not to me. And you—"

He touched her lips with her fingers. "Please, Deirdre."

She looked away from him again. "Leave me alone," she whispered.

Her eyes were closed, but he knew she was still conscious and able to listen to him. But he did not know what he could say or do to make her understand. He had never felt so helpless in his life. He had never known such torment as he knew now, looking at her, hurt and helpless, because of what he had done.

"Deirdre, listen to me. Don't turn away from me, honey. He was going to kill you. I had to do it. I had to take the chance, don't you understand? I'm sorry you got mixed up in it—I had men here to protect you, because this man wanted to hurt me through you. He's dangerous and he's got to be stopped. I'm not important and neither are you, compared to the damage and destruction he may do. I had to stop him, even if it cost—at whatever cost," he said gently. "He was counting on the fact that I would do as he asked to save you. But I knew he meant nothing he said. I knew he would fire, anyway. I had to call his bluff."

"You didn't care if he killed me," Deirdre whispered.

"It isn't that," he said desperately. "Deirdre, you know I love you. I know I'm doing a poor job at explaining it, but you've got to understand. I'd give anything if I could have prevented this happening. We were lucky. You're going to be all right. We'll still get him. Now, look, don't try to answer me now. I'll see you tomorrow. You're going to a hospital, and when you feel better, we'll talk about it."

She turned her head to look at him again. Her eyes were

cold and remote. Her face was a mask of cameo. Her lips moved for a moment before she spoke.

"I don't ever want to see you again, Sam. Not ever again." She closed her eyes. "We're finished. Forever and for good. I know the meaning of your love now, and I don't want any part of that kind of love. Don't come to see me. I don't want to talk any more. Just go away now. Go on with your hunting. That's what you're really anxious to do right now."

He heard a siren keening distantly in the night. The front door opened and closed, and Lew Franklin came into the library and paused, his young face lean and sober. Durell straightened, wincing as his arm gave him a sudden stab of pain.

"Any sign of Korvuth?"

"Not yet," Franklin said. He kept looking at Deirdre. "Is she going to be all right?"

"Of course." Durell's voice was suddenly harsh. Then it softened. "You look beat, Lew. Stay here with her. The ambulance is coming. See that she gets the best of care, will you? I'm going out after him."

"You could use a doctor yourself," Franklin said.

"Later."

He went out, aware of the strange look on Franklin's face as he stared at Deirdre again. It had finally stopped raining, but the night was cold and dark and dripping wet, with an icy wind blowing from the east, over the Chesapeake. Nobody had touched Zoltan Ske's body. Durell walked past it, down the path and into the woods to the north, bordering the cove. He drew in long, deep breaths of the icy air and told himself that Deirdre was shocked right now and not sure of what she had said, and it would be all right tomorrow. It had to be all right between them. He had to make her understand why he had risked her life in order to try for Korvuth. He told himself he could do this, and yet one dark part of his mind kept telling him that he had lost her forever.

It was an effort to turn his attention back to Korvuth. He halted just inside the pine woods and tried to put himself in the other man's place. A narrow path meandered through the wet pines toward the water's edge and he moved that way, his gun in hand, aware of a growing weakness in him from his own wound. But there was no time to think about himself. From his left, inland, came the flickering of flashlights as George Mester was joined by Art Greenwald's crew. In a few more minutes there would be a dozen, maybe a score of men joining the search. But Korvuth had escaped this sort of cordon before, and there was no reason to think he couldn't do it again. He had spent over ten minutes with Deirdre— time enough for anyone with training to get away.

He called to George Mester and moved toward the lights. A narrow dirt road, frozen hard, ran northward along the edge of the woods, and it was here that the searching men were gathering, trying to establish a cordon to keep Korvuth bottled in against the shore. A car came along fast, and three more men from the Maryland State Police joined the search. Durell put Mester in charge and struck off alone toward the waterfront. Some of what Deirdre had said to him was true. He felt in him a deep and sullen rage, a lust to kill. His objectivity was gone. He wanted Korvuth for himself now. Nothing else would satisfy him. And for this reason he wanted to search alone, following the hunch that teased the back of his mind.

The bullet hole in his arm had stopped bleeding, but he had to hold himself carefully. The path toward the waterfront twisted and turned between the soughing, dripping masses of pines. Now and then the wind strengthened and a shower of icy water drenched him, and he shivered with the chill. When he came out on the rough shingle of the beach, the wind from the open Chesapeake cut bitterly through his wet clothing.

There was no sign that anyone had passed this way, but that did not necessarily mean anything. He turned north, moving in the shadows of the pines until he came to a swampy area that he knew was a favorite spot for duck hunters. Several old blinds had been built along the waterfront here, visible now through the brittle reeds growing along the ice-crusted shore, and Durell checked each one carefully before going on. The path led inland for a short distance and then came out again on the shore, this time to the north of the cove. Tom Yordie's pungy was still out there, its riding light dimly visible through the laced pattern of brittle weeds. Apparently it was at anchor, because he couldn't hear the sound of the old engine. He could see no one aboard, either.

The Prince John Gun Club used this area occasionally, and its members had built a shelter hut over on the far point. Durell had walked here with Deirdre many times, and he knew the ground well. A stretch of swamp, often inundated with tidal water, served as a barrier between the shelter hut and the more solid land to the west, where the search was going on. Durell looked back, but the lights of the searching men were obscured by the trees. He held his gun a little higher and walked through the cold darkness to the point.

Without a torch to guide him, he had to move with care, and slowly, through the black night. Only a faint, luminous glow to the north, from the street lights of Prince John village, broke the utter darkness, but the reflected light from the low, scudding clouds only served to make shapeless shadows and strange patterns out of the land and the bay, the massed swamp oaks and pines and the dully glistening expanse of the Chesapeake. Durell moved forward to within twenty yards of the shelter hut before his straining eyes identified its vague shape against the deeper blackness of the night. A small, rickety wharf projected into the cove, and two skiffs had been pulled up and overturned on the shingle nearby. Durell looked out at the anchored pungy, then at the low, looming bulk of the shelter hut. Suddenly he was sure he had come to the right place. Korvuth was here. He was somewhere nearby. Every instinct told him this, and he stood very still, watching and listening, hearing the lap of icy water against the shore, the sigh of the wind, the brittle clashing of branches behind him. His training urged him to go back for help. But he wanted Korvuth for himself. This was something that had to be settled between the two of them.

Nothing moved in the windy darkness. He stepped forward again, closing the distance toward the hut. Now he saw that one of the skiffs on the beach beside the pier was not overturned, but rode on the tide, moored with a line to one of the pier pilings. His pulse quickened, and he turned back to the shack.

The shot and the scream of warning came simultaneously.

The muzzle flare came spitting from the hut. The scream seemed to echo from the shadows under the pier. Durell threw himself flat. The voice that had warned him was a woman's, and it came again, sharp and clear. He did not understand the words. She seemed to be talking to the man with the gun who had been waiting for him. Talking to Korvuth, in rapid, bitter Hungarian. A curse answered her. Another shot cracked the silence wide open. From far away, beyond the tongue of marsh that almost made an island of the point, came the alarmed yells of the searching troopers.

Durell was pinned down on the beach. There was agony in his arm and shoulder, because he had dropped instinctively, without thought for his wound. It was bleeding again, and for a moment the earth heaved and turned under him.

"This way!" the woman called.

He did not think he could get up. A wave of weakness kept him on his belly on the beach. He looked up and someone was running from the hut, back toward the dark swamps. He got his gun up with an effort and fired once, twice. His vision was blurred. The woman called out to him again and he got to his hands and knees and tried to stand. He had missed. The running man, Korvuth, was gone. He did not understand what was happening, but he turned toward the beach. His legs were like rubber, and he felt the warmth of his blood running alarmingly down his arm and off his fingertips. The girl came toward him, up the slope of the beach, with a gun in her hand. She wore a red hat. She was the girl who had followed him from New York.

"Oh, you fool," she said. "You let him get away!"

"Ilona?"

"Who did you think?" she said bitterly. She came close to him, her gun held warily, and he could see the anger in her face. "What is the matter with you? Are you hurt?"

There was a strange roaring sound in Durell's ears. He tried to reach for her gun and his hand went wavering off to one side and he looked at it in surprise before he felt his legs slowly buckle and he pitched forward and down.

Chapter Seven

FOR SOME TIME there was darkness, and a strange mechanical creaking sound, and a feeling that the world had become a queasy, unsettled place, without stability or solidity. He felt hands on him and heard the girl's voice talking, and he listened to learn if someone answered her, but no one did and he guessed she was talking to herself, bitterly and angrily. He felt himself being pushed and hauled and once the pain in his shoulder became so great that the darkness swallowed him again for several long minutes, and when he opened his eyes again he was not sure what time it was or where he could be. He felt a vibration all through his body, as if an engine were running and shaking the bunk on which he lay on his back, and he looked up at the silvery light that seemed to have no earthly point of origin. This last was correct, because he turned his head and looked out of a small porthole and saw that the wind had scoured the sky clean and a half-moon was shining, cold and distant and bleak, upon a waste of water, reaching everywhere in the small arc that he could see beyond the glass. He was on a boat, and he was sure it was the pungy.

He turned his head and looked at the bunk on the other side of the narrow cabin. An old man sat there looking at him. Durell had never seen the man before. Shaggy gray hair, shaggy beard, a weathered face like ancient leather, bright eyes alert with curiosity under massive eyebrows. The old man had no teeth, and he mouthed his gums a moment before he spoke.

"Feel pretty sick, hey, young feller?"

"I've felt better."

"She took pretty good care of you, son. Right smart girl. Kind of frightening, in a way. Ain't used to women like that no more."

"Are you Tom Yordie?" Durell asked. "This is your boat?"

The old man nodded. "She come out in the skiff and hauled you aboard. Made me help, at the point of a gun. Then she used my medicine kit to take care of that bullet hole in you. You were lucky, young feller. The slug went in and out, clean as a whistle. No trouble at all. She knew what she was doing." The old man chuckled. "Here, have a nip of this. Made it myself. Always prefer my own mix."

Yordie extended a gnarled, rope-hardened hand with an old brown bottle. Durell took it, nodded thanks, and swallowed deeply. The liquor was not unlike the mule he had known long ago, back in the bayous. It exploded warmly in the pit of his stomach and spread its heat through his body. He looked at his shoulder and saw that a neat bandage covered the wound. He looked for his gun. It was gone. Tom Yordie grinned.

"She thinks of everything. We're halfway across the bay by now, and them roosters on the shore ain't got the foggiest idea you're here. You gonna tell me what this is all about, young feller?"

"I thought you might know," Durell said flatly.

"Don't know nothing. Go on, drink up. I can always make more." Tom Yordie watched Durell take another long swallow of the white liquor. "You drink like you're used to the stuff. I like that. Some of them namby-pamby Washington folk come out here to hunt an' fish, they fancy their own liquors. Like water. Can't stand the stuff."

"You haven't answered my question," Durell said.

"All I know is some feller come rowing out to my boat late in the day an' when I invite him aboard, he rewards me with a crack on the head. I wake up tied up and alone, until the girl shows up, maybe an hour ago. She looks at me and then she goes back ashore and then she comes back with you. That's all. She untied me when she needed help hoistin' you in. You're a pretty fair load, even for her."

"Where is she now?" Durell asked.

"At the wheel."

Durell swung his legs off the bunk and stood up. The tiny cabin had a low overhead, and he had to duck, clinging to the bunks on either side. Tom Yordie didn't offer to help him. He had to sit down again after the first try, aware of a cool moisture breaking out all over his body. He took a deep breath and stood up again. This time he remained on his feet.

"You a cop?" Yordie asked suddenly.

"No."

"Rob a bank?"

"No. Stay here." Durell made his way to the small hatch and ladder leading up to the stern deck. For a few moments he did not think he would get up the steps. He was weaker than he thought. Then he drew a deep breath and pushed the hatch open and stepped out into the night wind.

They were two or three miles offshore. A deep swell was running with the incoming tide, and the pungy pitched in the uneasy current as it quartered against the thrust of the seas. The wind was cold and sharp, but it had scoured the skies until the stars and the moon were out, and he could see the distant mass of the Maryland shore, the cluster of town lights a little to the south, the regular flash of a beacon not far away. Durell braced himself against the pitch of the deck and looked at the girl. She stood easily at the wheel, watching him, her figure only a slight, dark outline against the stars. Then he saw the gun in her hand.

"Do not come too close to me, please," she said.

He saw that she had tied the skiff astern and was towing it. He did not go near her. In the moonlight she looked young and defenseless, but he knew that this was an illusion; her shoulders were straight, her stance alert, and the face she turned toward him was a mask that was neither friendly nor inimical.

"How do you feel now?"

"Tom Yordie's corn helped. You helped, too. Korvuth

might have killed me back there on the beach. You yelled and startled him and he took off. Why did you do it?"

"Perhaps I've had enough of killing," she said quietly. "Sit down over there. I don't trust you."

"You don't trust me, but you saved my life and then hauled me out here. Kidnaping, practically." Durell's laugh was dry. "You patched me up, got me into a bunk, and sailed out into the middle of the Chesapeake. All this, after following me from New York. Can you tell me why?"

"I want to talk to you. I know who you are, you see."

"All right, go ahead and talk."

"It is rather confusing. I am not sure what course of action I should take. But I do not like that old man to hear anything of what I have to say to you. Our talk must be strictly confidential. So I think we should get rid of him."

Durell said flatly: "He hasn't done anything to hurt you. He's just a harmless old fisherman."

She looked at him with bleak eyes. "I am not a monster. I do not intend to kill him, as you seem to think. But he is strong for an old man, and he can easily row ashore from here in the skiff."

"So we get rid of him. And then?"

"We talk. I can help you, although it is dangerous for me. And you can help me."

Durell looked at the skiff and then at the distant shore. It was not too far. There was a bite of decision and command in the girl's voice, and a way she held her gun, that made him shrug and raise no objections. Curiosity moved in him, more powerful than the sense of defeat and frustration he had felt a few moments before. There were enough men on shore to take care of the hunt for Korvuth.

He nodded, and the girl said, "Get him."

It took no more than five minutes for Tom Yordie to climb into the skiff, ship his oars, and begin his long row for shore. The old man raised no objections. Once he started to ask a question, then looked at the girl's face and the gun in her hand and shrugged his bowed shoulders in resignation. He spoke to Durell as he climbed into the skiff. "Take care of my boat, young feller. I don't know who you are, or what's happenin' rightly, but this boat is all I got in the world. It's my home, and I don't want her wrecked. You'll look after her?"

"Sure," Durell said.

"I left you the rest of that bottle." He looked at the girl again. "I reckon you might need it, at that."

When he was gone, a small bowed figure bent to the oars of the little skiff, Durell turned back to the girl. "You understand that he will call the police as soon as he gets ashore?"

"It will be several hours until then. The matters we must discuss will be decided by that time." The girl turned the switch on the wheezing old engine, and the pungy was suddenly quiet except for the lapping of water along its white sides. The boat lifted and fell, drifting easily on the tidal current. "I do not think it will be dangerous for us if we simply allow the wind to push us," she said. "I am cold and I could use a drink. Let us go below and talk." She moved her gun. "After you, Mr. Durell."

He went down into the tiny cabin, found the bottle Yordie had left, handed it to her, and then sat down on one of the bunks. It was cold aboard now, with no heating equipment in the cabin with the engine off, and only the planks of the hull to fend off the icy wind blowing over the bay. In the dim overhead light he saw the girl clearly for the first time. She took off the red felt hat and shook her coppery hair free, and he saw it was long and silken, more than shoulder-length. Her face with its prominent cheekbones might have been beautiful except for the lines of exhaustion marked around her mouth and the violet shadows under her dark-brown eyes. Little flecks of gold shone in them as she sat down, the gun beside her on the bunk, and took the bottle from him. She still wore the woolen skirt and sweater and the tweed coat he had seen her in before.

She drank and coughed and he could have taken the gun from her then, but he did not move. She looked up and smiled. "There is no subtlety in American liquor, is there?"

"It's home brew," he said. "Tom Yordie's own mash. People get to like it, after a while."

"Another example of American individuality and independence?"

"You could call it that," he said. "You speak English well. Were you trained in Moscow?"

"Of course. I expected you to recognize that."

"You did a poor job of shadowing me," he told her.

"I wanted you to see me and know where I was."

"Have you split with Bela Korvuth?"

She nodded slowly. "It is definite now. I could not stand it. So much has happened, in only one day." She ignored the gun beside her and clasped her hands together in her lap and leaned forward toward him. She shivered a little. "I can help you, Mr. Durell. But you must help me in return. That is why I needed this private conference with you. Anywhere else, it would be dangerous. Korvuth would find us, or you would not listen. Here, you and I can talk as two people, apart from everything else."

"I'm willing to listen."

"Of course. We know all about you. I thought you would prefer to talk. We consider you one of the most dangerous men against us. I do not know if what I have done so far is right. Perhaps I will be killed for it and perhaps I will deserve it. I will not lie to you. I came over here as part of Korvuth's apparatus, to kill you, to get you off our books."

"That wasn't all of your job," he said.

"No. Not all of it. Neither was Endre Stryzyk." She shuddered, and for a moment she looked as if she were going to be sick. Durell reached across the narrow cabin and simply picked the gun off the bunk beside her. She did not move or object. All at once she made a sound of sickness in her throat and stood up and went quickly up the hatch to the deck again. Durell pocketed the gun and sat quietly, waiting for her. His shoulder throbbed, but she had done almost a professional job on the bandaging. His arm would be stiff for a few days, but if he could get a shot of penicillin soon, it shouldn't trouble him too much. He waited for the girl to come back.

She looked subdued, almost shy, when she climbed down the ladder into the cabin again. She was shivering violently, and he got one of the blankets and put it around her, awkward because of his arm, and then closed the hatch tightly against the wind. The boat rolled with an easy motion now, moving with the tide.

"I am sorry," the girl whispered. Her American accent was almost perfect, a tribute to her training. "Everything has gone wrong for me, and today has been a nightmare. I saw things I did not believe possible. In New York, in New Jersey, on the train—everywhere. It was so different from what I had been told it would be like."

"Suppose you tell me why you fell out with Bela Korvuth." She looked surprised. "Because of Endre, of course."

"The farmhand in Jersey? The one Bela killed?"

"There was no need to kill him—no reason at all!" she whispered bitterly. "It was a vicious, senseless act. I—I knew Endre back in Budapest, you see. We went to school together. I knew his family."

Durell was quiet. He knew that this was the first break in the whole thing—something unexpected and unlooked for, and his mind jumped ahead coolly, planning to exploit it. She looked like a lost, forlorn child, huddled in the blanket—not a woman any more, not dangerous. Just a lost, frightened human being, betrayed and hopeless. Drifting as surely as the pungy drifted, without rhyme or reason, without a rudder or a motive to set a course.

"You knew that Endre was with the freedom fighters," he said.

"Yes, we knew them all, mostly. Endre was a good boy, though. There was nothing mean about him. He was always joking, always laughing—until his father was arrested last year. We had to arrest the old man; he wouldn't change. He was stubborn, foolishly clinging to the old ways—" Ilona paused and looked up, a look of shock in her eyes changed by a wry little smile that curved her mouth downward. She kneaded her hands together. "It is terrible, what they make of one. A robot, mouthing empty phrases. It is still in me, even after today. They hammer and hammer at you, until you repeat and shout the slogans that have no meaning. But there was no reason to kill Endre today. None at all." She shook her head violently and looked down. Durell could not see her face. Her long, dark-red hair screened her cheek as she turned her head partly away from him. She was struggling hard, trying not to cry. He wished she would let it all go but he knew better than to put pressure on her. It was only the solitude of being alone on this boat with him, temporarily safe and isolated from the world, that enabled her to talk at all. Her next words surprised him. "I'm so hungry," she whispered.

"Haven't you eaten today?"

"Nothing at all. Not since breakfast."

"And your clothes are wet from the rain before."

She shivered. "You are no better off than I."

He got up off the bunk. He felt better now, stronger. Maybe it was Tom Yordie's liquor, or the expert attention the girl had given to his wound. It didn't matter. She looked ill, half frozen, hungry, troubled and uncertain in her mind. There was a small galley forward, and her told her to get out of her clothes while he was there and stay wrapped in the blanket, and then he found some cans of soup and primed the little alcohol stove and began heating the soup in a pan. He waited five minutes for her to do as he said, and when he returned, she had strung her wet woolen skirt and her stockings and briefs on a line between the bunks and sat huddled again in the blanket. Her smile was shy.

"You can be kind," she said. "It is not what they told us about you."

"Am I supposed to be some kind of an ogre?"

"A tool of the capitalistic warmongers. A methodical killer." Durell laughed. "And you believed it?"

"I believed everything, until today."

"Until Korvuth killed Endre Stryzyk?"

"Yes. Until then. He was a good boy. He fought for what he thought was right. And perhaps he was right. I am too confused now to know black from white. Anyway, his people lost, and he ran away. He was entitled to be left in peace, having given up the struggle. He was hurting no one here. And I keep remembering how things were in school—"

"Were you in love with Endre?" Durell asked.

"No, no. It was nothing like that. We were just friends." Her eyes widened slowly, remembering. "He kept looking at me, under that bridge, when Korvuth made him get out of the truck this morning. He remembered me, all right. But he could not believe I would let Korvuth kill him—not until the last moment. And then he looked at me in a way I wish I could forget, but which I will never get out of my mind. And he said something—he said I was dead, too. Worse than dead. And he cursed me. And then Korvuth laughed and—killed him." She looked up again, hugging the blanket around her body. Her face was tormented. "Please. I am trusting you. We can help each other, you and I. But you look ill, Mr. Durell. You have been hurt. Your clothes are wet, too."

"All right," he said.

He went into the galley and stripped, listening for sounds from her, but the boat, rocking idly in the tidal current, was quiet except for the soothing lap of the sea running along the planking, and an occasional whimper of the cold wind. It felt warmer in the cabin, and he found a coarse towel and rubbed himself down and hung up his damp clothing. There was another blanket in the storage lockers in the galley, and he wrapped it around himself clumsily, saving his injured arm, and went back to the Hungarian girl. She had not moved. She had found a cigarette and sat holding it, looking at something he could not see, staring at a horror he did not know.

"Ilona, you'd better just answer my questions," he said. "We'll get ahead further that way."

"I'm so cold," she whispered.

"Finish the soup."

"I can't swallow it."

He sat down on the bunk beside her. "Korvuth and Zoltan Ske and you were sent over here as a team, weren't you?"

"Yes."

"Somebody in our Austrian offices helped you get through our immigration checks, didn't he?"

"I suppose so. I don't know the details."

"Dunstermeir, in Jersey, was one of your contacts?"

"Yes."

"But you didn't know Endre Stryzyk was there?"

"I think Korvuth knew. But I never suspected—"

"All right," he said quickly. "Don't think about Endre right now. It's enough that he made you see the truth about things. You want to help us now, don't you?"

"Yes. There is nothing else for me to do. I couldn't go on with Bela—not after that, not after seeing what he did. If it had been necessary, for our mission, I might have understood."

"Just what is your mission, Ilona?"

She looked at him. Her dark brown eyes were wide. "To kill you, Mr. Durell."

"And who else?"

She shivered and was silent, struggling with herself. Durell felt impatient, but he curbed the questions in him and waited her out. She made a small sound and shook her head. "I feel as though I am doing wrong."

"By talking to me?"

"It is a matter of training and habit." She sighed. "All my life I worked for the State. I have known nothing else. The war and the Russian occupation happened when I was a child. But when I saw the people fighting and rioting, when I saw that it was only by Soviet tanks firing on the working men and women of Budapest, and when the Mongolian troops came into my city to crush and kill and stamp upon and terrorize . . . when I saw the hatred, Mr. Durell—" She paused again and swallowed. There was a clean, clear attraction to her face, Durell thought, now that she had lost her dedicated, efficient look. She was only a frightened, confused girl, not knowing where to turn. "Korvuth was sent over here to kill you, Mr. Durell. But that was only a side issue. His real aim was to kill or kidnap Dr. Anton Tagy."

"Tagy?" The name meant nothing. "Anton Tagy?"

"He is working for you as a physicist. A Hungarian, one of my people, who escaped when the Russians came in first, years ago. I believe he is in California now. It is known by us that he has solved, or nearly solved, the problem of using the hydrogen bomb reaction for peaceful purposes. The Russians want to know this, too. They want the information from him. It is Korvuth's mission to find Dr. Tagy and get that information or stop his work for you."

"But that's not all," Durell said.

She looked up quickly. In the dim glow of the lamp in the cabin overhead, she looked startled. "You are very clever."

"The other mission is to set up a sabotage ring among the stooges you managed to slip through among the innocent refugees, isn't that so?"

"Yes," she said, nodding.

"You know the names of the members of this apparatus?"

"No. Only Korvuth knows. He has memorized them."

"He never mentioned any of them?"

"No. Believe me. He never did. I was only a very minor member of the group organization. Perhaps Zoltan Ske, if you caught him—"

"We caught him. He's dead," Durell said grimly.

She made another small sound. "I am not sorry."

"What else do you know about Dr. Tagy?" he asked.

"Nothing. Only his name, really; his reputation. That is all."

Durell got up and went into the galley and took a damp pack of cigarettes from his trousers hanging there, lit two of them, and returned to give Ilona one. She inhaled gratefully, then looked up and smiled, shyly again. "You do not know what this hour has meant. Peace. And safety. Even though it is only an illusion."

"I'll help you, Ilona. You won't have to be afraid any more."

"I want to stay in this country."

"I'll see that it's arranged that way."

Then her eyes darkened, the gold flecks fading in the deep brown. "No. I have a feeling it will not be the way I wish. You do not know the kind of man Bela Korvuth is. He is a monster. I was always a little afraid of him, when I would see him in the AVO offices, in Budapest. There is something about him that makes the flesh creep, the blood run cold— the way he looks at you, not as one human looks at another, but as if you were a specimen of some strange form of life, whose fate is unimportant to the master scheme he works for." She looked down at her hands. The blanket had slipped from her shoulders, and Durell saw that her skin was smooth and fair. "I am afraid of him. He will kill me. He knows I have deserted him, because I helped you a little while ago. He will hunt me down. He will always be a shadow behind me, until he does what he wants."

"We know all about Bela Korvuth," Durell said. "We won't let him touch you."

The girl watched him in silence as he stood up again. It was almost midnight. His head ached, and he felt cold, but he got his clothing in the tiny galley and dressed, resenting the clammy touch of the damp wool. There was a dull pulsing in his arm, and he held his side stiffly to keep the wound from bleeding again. A vision of Deirdre moved through his mind. He lit a cigarette and told himself she would be all right; she *had* to be all right. And when she felt herself again, she would listen to him and understand that he had done what had to be done. She would know he hadn't wanted it; she would realize he would rather a hundred times take the pain and danger for himself, rather than have her so much as scratched.

He heard a sound from the narrow doorway to the galley and the redheaded girl squeezed in quickly, then pressed back against the weathered and worn bulkhead. Her eyes were somber, dark.

"I have been selfish. I meant to ask—about your woman. Did Bela reach her? Did he—"

"She's badly injured," Durell said shortly.

"I am sorry. Very sorry."

"We'll go back now, Ilona."

She nodded slowly, caught her lower lip in small, white teeth. "Yes, I can see you must. Do not look at me like that, Mr. Durell. I did not want Bela Korvuth to hurt her."

The pungy lifted and fell in the tidal current. The girl swayed, lost her balance, and caught at him for support with a murmur of apology. Her blanket fell away and for a moment he glimpsed her slender, lithe body before she caught it up again. She flushed. "I had better dress, too. You have my gun. I have surrendered myself to you. Am I under arrest, Mr. Durell?"

"We'll discuss it in Washington," he said.

She nodded and went back into the cabin for her clothing. Durell leaned against the galley cabinets and smoked his cigarette. His face was hard and bleak. There was so much to do, and so little time in which to do it. He kept seeing Deirdre's face, and heard her voice reject him as she turned away from him. He looked at his hands and saw they were shaking a little. He needed a doctor for himself. He needed sleep, rest, several days in bed.

But there was so little time.

Chapter Eight

DURELL reached his bachelor's apartment in Washington at almost four o'clock in the morning. He had checked the hospital where Deirdre had been taken and learned that she was resting comfortably after an emergency operation to remove the bullet. After that he had taken Ilona to No. 20 Annapolis Street, headquarters for K Section of the CIA, and sat in on an emergency session there in the innocent-appearing graystone building that bore a plaque indicating it was the office headquarters of a commercial enterprise. Several facts emerged from the meeting, the primary one being that Bela Korvuth had again eluded the men Durell had hastily organized for a search throughout the Prince John area. Korvuth had once more vanished into thin air, with the elusiveness of a fox. A routine inquiry was sent through AEC channels to contact Dr. Tagy, at the California laboratory of UCLA, where his experiments were being conducted. AEC Security was peculiarly tight-lipped about the inquiry, promising nothing, and Durell was too tired to press it at four in the morning. A coded message was sent to Dickinson McFee in London. Ilona was held in custody. There was an apartment on the top floor of No. 20 Annapolis Street designed for such transient purposes, and Durell saw to it that she was made comfortable there.

"Will you come back tomorrow?" she asked Durell.

"First thing. Don't worry, now. Get some rest."

"Will I be imprisoned? Or executed?"

"Executed? We don't do things that way over here."

She smiled wanly. "I won't worry if you promise to help me."

When he left her, he submitted to the attentions of a

medical officer summoned to the dispensary. His wound was probed, sterilized, and bandaged again, and he was ordered to stay in bed for a week. Durell didn't argue with the doctor about it. He went home.

He slept restlessly. He got up at ten and took a hot shower, feeling awkward because of the bandages on his shoulder that kept his arm stiff, and made his own breakfast in his kitchenette, bacon, eggs, and a strong pot of Louisiana coffee. The shoulder holster did not fit well over the bandages when he dressed, and he settled it by keeping the snubby-barreled .38 in his pocket. The telephone rang while he was drinking his third cup of coffee. It was Sanderson, temporary sub-chief at K Section.

"Sam? Can you get down right away?"

"I was just coming," Durell said. "Anything kicking?"

"Joint Chiefs. And AEC. The boss himself is at the White House. How do you feel?"

"Like the product of a meat grinder."

Sanderson said: "Well, we might get along without you, Cajun—"

"I'll be there."

He hung up and finished his coffee. It was a bright winter day in Washington. Yesterday's storm was gone and the sky was a pale, flawless blue. He finished dressing, wearing a sober blue suit, a button-down white shirt, and a dark figured maroon necktie. When he took a long look at himself in the mirror, he did not like what he saw. He kept hearing Deirdre's whispered, broken accusations, and he kept seeing the remoteness in her eyes when she had looked at him last night. Before he went out, he telephoned the hospital and asked for Deirdre Padgett's condition. The nurse sounded cheerful.

"Very good this morning. Would you like to speak to her?"

"Yes, please. Tell her it's Durell."

There was a long pause, a few vague sounds in the receiver, and then the nurse came back on the telephone. "I'm terribly sorry, Mr. Durell."

"What is it? Can't she talk?"

"She would rather not. Miss Padgett asked me to tell you not to telephone again."

"Look, I—"

"I'm so sorry, sir."

He hung up. There was a florist's shop in the lobby of his apartment house, and he stopped in there and ordered a dozen roses sent to the hospital. He debated sending a card along with it, and rejected the idea, and then walked around the corner to the parking lot and got his car and drove to Annapolis Street. The day did not seem as bright as it had.

Sidonie Osbourn was at the outer desk in his office. She was a small, pert French girl, the widow of an agent Durell had worked with as a partner two years ago, before Lew was killed. Durell and Deirdre were frequent visitors to her small, neat home in an Alexandria suburb, and Durell was always warmly welcomed by Sidonie's twin girls. But he found no warmth or welcome in Sidonie's large, questioning eyes this morning.

He smiled. "You here, too, on Sunday, Sid?"

"Top priority meeting. They're waiting for you, Sam."

"Another moment or two won't tarnish their brass."

She looked down at her typewriter, unsmiling. "As you wish."

He paused. "What is it, Sidonie? Why the cold shoulder?"

"You ought to know, Sam."

"Because of Deirdre? You think I wanted her to get hurt?"

Sidonie began typing furiously. "I don't want to discuss it. I'm sure you saw your duty and did it."

"Look," he said, "have you seen Deirdre this morning?"

"I was at the hospital all night. Where were you?"

He started to reply, then closed his mouth in a hard, angry line. There was no way he could combat the cold, aloof set of her slim shoulders. He went to the window and looked down at the Sunday peace and calm of Annapolis Street. No town in the world could go as dead and quiet as Washington on a Sunday. For once, there was no overt international crisis to disrupt the embassies or the huge State Department building. He knew the people here at K Section had arrived singly and unobtrusively, since not even the residents of the neighboring buildings had any inkling of the true function of No. 20 Annapolis. He lit a cigarette and again started to speak to Sidonie, then decided there was no point to arguing the matter now. He went on up to the third floor, walking with a long, angry stride. The communications center was manned, and he heard the pinging of a teletype machine and the humming of a computer in the Analysis and Synthesis Department as the weekly summary was prepared for Joint Chiefs. The conference was in McFee's office, and he nodded to Alex, the brawny young security guard there, and went in.

Fred Holcomb sat at McFee's desk, a chunky, middle-aged man who smoked a stubby pipe and who looked perpetually worried. Holcomb was a synthesis man, in charge of compiling the weekly estimate of world conditions out of the hundred of reports from all the corners of the world. He looked out of his medium in Dickinson McFee's small, simple office.

"Good morning, Sam," he nodded. "How do you feel?"

"Like I've been shot. Are we ready?"

"Sure. I'm sorry about Deirdre, Sam." There was a reservation in Fred's voice, too, and in his manner. His eyes shifted away from Durell's tall figure and he introduced the others in the room. Patten, from State, McGregor, FBI, a general named Jackson from Pentagon and an unobtrusive, quiet little man representing the White House. Durell felt a prickle of apprehension as he looked at their faces. Something important must have broken to warrant this sort of a meeting. He sensed the same peculiar reserve in their manner as they looked at him, as if he were an object of curiosity, an attitude that was somewhat the same as he had received from Sidonie Osbourn.

Holcomb rapped the dottle of his pipe and cleared his throat. "We've had some interesting news overnight, Sam. Rather serious, to say the least. Since McFee put you in charge, we thought you ought to be here to listen in."

"I haven't dropped the matter," Durell said.

"Your orders are to rest for a week," Holcomb said.

"I'll use my own discretion about that. What happened?"

McGregor, the FBI man, said: "To put it bluntly, your inquiry about Dr. Tagy surprised us. We thought we had kept the matter quiet. We didn't want to give our opponents the opportunity of making propaganda capital out of another defection from our scientific ranks." McGregor was tall and lanky, with a soft voice and a pleasant, tanned face. "Dr. Tagy disappeared from his laboratories almost two months ago."

Durell nodded. "And you haven't picked up any trace of him?"

"We have a pretty good idea of where he's gone. Back to Hungary. He has a wife and son in Budapest. We checked his associates carefully to find out if he had been worried about them. It seems that since the uprising in Hungary, he's been able to talk of nothing else. It's a pretty fair guess that he somehow managed to go back to them, maybe to try to get them out of the country. But there hasn't been a sign of him anywhere. If he's in Budapest, he's managed to stay well hidden. You say this Bela Korvuth came over here to get him. It could be ironic. Obviously, their secret police don't know that Tagy is missing. They couldn't know he's back in their bailiwick, or they wouldn't have sent Korvuth here to nab him or wipe him."

"You sound reasonably sure Dr. Tagy is in Budapest, though."

McGregor shrugged. "It's only an assumption, naturally. We traced him to Mexico, and then to Havana, and then to a Greek freighter bound for Athens. After that—nothing. I can tell you this, though. We want him back. He's needed here; his work is damned important. His associates have tried to finish the lab tests on the experimental lines he laid down for utilizing the hydrogen reaction for power production, but they're just floundering. Nothing has come of it, and nothing will, unless Dr. Tagy comes back of his own accord, or somebody goes over there to bring him back."

Durell said flatly: "That can be arranged. We won't have to worry about Korvuth for a short time, anyway. Maybe a decoy can be set up in the university labs to keep Korvuth from suspecting Dr. Tagy isn't there."

"We've already arranged for that, Sam," Holcomb said. "There's one other thing you ought to know, though." Holcomb looked around at the other silent men in the room. He looked harassed and worried, and he picked up his pipe and fumbled with it for a moment and then put it aside with a decisive motion. "Dickinson McFee went to Europe yesterday about this thing. About Dr. Tagy, I mean. We didn't know at the time, of course, that Dr. Tagy was Korvuth's objective. But since the two cases tie in, you're in it now, too. McFee was going to Vienna to see what he could do about locating Tagy and persuading him to come back— maybe help him get his wife and son out of Budapest, if possible."

"Why didn't he send someone to do the job?" Durell asked. "It isn't like McFee to take to the field himself, these days."

Holcomb shrugged. "In Vienna, he was going to look for the leak that let Korvuth and the people of his apparatus slip through our check lines. He had a feeling it was too delicate to trust to anyone else. He wanted to look around for himself, working out of our Vienna Embassy, before probing Budapest for Dr. Tagy." Holcomb cleared his throat nervously. "When you reported Bela Korvuth's objective last night, I cabled London to advise General McFee. He had already arrived and changed planes for Vienna. At least, that's what Waterman, our London man, said. So I checked Vienna. Less than an hour ago, Sam. McFee arrived there, all right, and he went straight to the border. He hasn't been heard from since."

There was silence in the somber, brown office. Durell felt the eyes of the other men in the room fixed on him. He looked at them in turn, angry at their objectivity, at the strange manner in which they regarded him. It could only be because of what had happened to Deirdre, he thought. They considered him something less than human. He heard Holcomb clear his throat again.

"It's in your lap, Sam. McFee left you in charge, and he gave you a free hand. He made that clear to me. Ordinarily, I don't go along with that kind of assignment. We're a team, and we're supposed to work together. You were hurt yesterday, and Deirdre—well, if you want to put someone else on this thing, we'll understand. You could use the rest."

"No," Durell said.

"You don't have to feel that any of it is your personal responsibility, Sam."

"It is. I want Korvuth for myself."

"There's nothing more you can do, though. The laboratory in California is supplied with a man who looks reasonably enough like Dr. Tagy. The place is staked out, and our people are ready. It's simply a waiting game, holding on until Bela Korvuth shows up out there."

"And if he doubles back for Budapest?"

"He doesn't know Dr. Tagy is missing."

"He can find out. Don't underestimate him." Durell stood up, a tall and angry man. His eyes were dark. "As long as it's understood that this one is mine, I'm going ahead with it. My way. I take it the girl, Ilona, is still in custody upstairs?"

"Yes, Sam. She doesn't know about Dr. Tagy's disappearance. We've questioned her carefully. It could be that she's sincere in wanting to switch sides, but we're not sure."

"Well, we'll find out," Durell said flatly. "I'm going to Vienna. If McFee has vanished, it's because he stumbled onto something over there that's too hot to hold. I agree with you, we can let Bela Korvuth run himself ragged looking for Tagy in California. It won't last long, because he's smart and he'll soon find out the true score. But it gives us a little time to work on the other end of the rope. Maybe four or five days. With luck, maybe a week. I'm going over there and find Tagy. And McFee."

Nobody said anything. He read disapproval, even surprise, on the grim faces that watched him. It didn't matter. McFee had made his instructions clear enough before taking off for Europe. It was within his discretion to act as he saw fit.

Holcomb gestured vaguely. "Sam, you're in no condition to—"

"I am. I'm going."

"About the girl—"

"I'll need Ilona with me. My Hungarian is rather rusty. Besides, she knows Budapest, and I don't. She's our best bet for finding Dr. Tagy. It has to be done fast, before Korvuth catches the scent and doubles back. It's a calculated risk, going back there with the girl, but if I'm willing to take it, you gentlemen should have no objections." Durell turned to the door and paused. "I'd appreciate it, Fred, if you could check with SAC and learn where I might hitch a ride on a jet for Europe."

Chapter Nine

DURELL drove to the hospital from the conference, through the Sunday calm of Washington's streets. It had taken twenty minutes of insistence before the others had yielded to his determination. There had been two lengthy telephone calls to State, and the man from the White House had also used a phone, speaking quietly to someone unidentified for five minutes before he hung up with a quiet nod. Durell had gone up to the small apartment on the top floor of No. 20 Annapolis and talked to Ilona while the issue was still in doubt. There was an extensive wardrobe in the rooms where she was held in custody, outfits of both men's and women's clothing, and he told the red-haired girl to pick a few inconspicuous items of dress and be ready for him when he returned.

"You trust me this far?" she asked quietly.

"Only if you're willing to go back to Budapest with me," he told her. "It will be more dangerous for you, if the AVO picks you up there, than it will be for me."

"I will not deny that I am afraid," she whispered. "I had hoped to stay here in this country."

"You'll come back with me after we're successful."

"And if we do not succeed?"

Durell shrugged, watching and weighing her. She had looked rested and relaxed from a night's sleep when he first came in, outfitted in a skirt and green sweater she had borrowed from the wardrobe. In the clear morning light he saw that her face was sensitive and delicate, with a rather wide, generous mouth that contradicted the trained wariness of her large brown eyes. She had smiled and been cheerful when he came in, and then as he explained what he wanted her to do, the lines of strain reappeared in her young face, and a shadow touched her expression.

"This is voluntary on your part, Ilona," Durell said. "Please don't think I'm putting any pressure on you to do it. On the contrary, you understand how much I trust you and believe in your new allegiance to democracy when I ask you to come with me. My life will be in your hands many times." He had smiled wryly. "I'm not the one to make speeches, Ilona. But I need you with me. You can help tremendously. If you think it's too dangerous for you, of course, you are free to stay here."

"And will I be put in prison?"

"I doubt it. You will be in protective custody, of course, until a thorough investigation has been made and various people are convinced you mean what you say about staying over here and making a new life for yourself in America."

"It is what I want," she said quietly. "But if I can help you, I will go back with you. If you promise to take me with you when you return."

"I promise," he had told her solemnly.

"Then I will get ready now."

Durell could only guess at what the decision had cost the girl. He had given her little time to think about it. Assuming her motives were what he hoped and believed them to be, she was literally walking back into the jaws of death with him. He wished he had had time to learn more about her, to know the sort of person she really was. Perhaps the change of heart she claimed to feels was purely an act to cover a deeper and deadlier motive. He couldn't be sure. You could never be sure, in his business. Yet he needed her, because time was important, and there was little hope that he could do what had to be done if he went alone.

He parked his car in the hospital parking area and went in

through the emergency entrance. The wind was cold. The Sunday quiet had pervaded the hospital corridors, too. The nurse at the reception desk looked at him curiously when he asked to see Deirdre Padgett, and she opened her mouth as if she were going to object; then she met Durell's dark gaze and shrugged and scribbled on a card and gave it to him, and he went up in the elevator to the fourth floor.

Art Greenwald was just coming out of the room as Durell turned the corridor corner. Rosalie, Art's wife, was with him. Greenwald was a chunky, dark-haired man and Rosalie was always plump and cheerful. Durell had worked with the electronics man for a long time, and had helped Art's brother in the Stella Marni case. They were close friends.

"Cajun, wait a minute," Art said. He looked embarrassed and glanced at Rosalie for support. "Does Deirdre know you're coming?"

"She ought to know me well enough to expect me."

"Sam, she's in a pretty bad frame of mind, right now. She feels as though you—as if you let her down." Art looked harassed. "Maybe you ought to wait a few days."

"I can't wait," Durell said. "I'm leaving the country, and I don't know when—or if—I'll be back."

"Sam, please," Rosalie murmured. "Spare yourself."

"I've got to talk to her," Durell said.

He went in and quietly closed the door behind him. Something wrenched inside him when he saw Deirdre's pale face and quiet figure on the hospital cot. His roses had arrived and they had not been rejected. Oxygen tanks stood by the bedside, and an intravenous glucose injection against shock was being administered. Durell moved around so that Deirdre could look at him, standing with his back to the bright window overlooking the barren little park across from the hospital.

"Hello, Dee. How do you feel?"

She looked at him as if he were a stranger.

He pulled a chair to the bedside. "May I sit down?"

Her eyes were dark and gray. "As you wish," she whispered.

"Dee, aren't you going to try to understand?"

"I understand everything."

"I don't think you do. What happened last night makes you think I can't possibly love you. But I do. More than I can ever tell you in words." Durell touched her hand. She drew it away and turned her head aside so he could not see her face. Her dark hair looked soft and glossy against the antiseptic white of her pillow slip. "You're going to be all right, Dee. There's nothing to worry about. It's the way you feel about me that's troubling me. There's nothing more important to me than you. Surely you know that."

"No. That's not true. You proved that last night," she murmured.

"There was nothing else I could do," he said helplessly. "Look, don't think about anything but getting well, right now. Don't shut me out for good. I have to go away, Dee. Abroad. I should be back in a week, with luck. I had to tell you this, so you'd know why I won't be able to see you."

"I don't care," she said. "Nothing will ever be the same."

"Yes, it will. I'll make it so."

She shook her head slowly and looked away from him again. A nurse opened the door and stood there, waiting, her face bland and impersonal. Durell thought of a dozen phrases to pursue his argument with Deirdre, to try to make her understand. He spoke none of them. Her face and her mind were closed against him. There was a finality to the way she looked at him that created an abyss that his pride could not cross. He stood up slowly.

"Wish me luck, anyway, Dee."

"Yes."

She was not interested. She had no questions about where he was going or what he was going to do. She did not want to see him again.

He drove his car back to his apartment and changed his clothes, choosing a suit of European make from which all the labels had been removed, an English shirt and necktie, a pair of Russian-made black shoes. He arranged for his car to be taken to the garage, drew the blinds in his rooms, washed the coffee pot and dishes from his breakfast. He worked quickly, trying not to think or remember Deirdre's face as he last saw it. He checked with Sanderson and learned that the SAC bomber for Germany would leave from Florida in four and a half hours. An MATS plane was ready and waiting at the Washington airport to take him down there with the girl, to make his connection. There was an urgency in him now as he ended his preparations and took a cab to Annapolis Street to pick up Ilona. It was as if all the little chores of preparation had closed door after door behind him.

The girl was ready and waiting. Her face was pale and set, and she walked quietly with him out of the sanctuary of Annapolis Street. She was silent in the cab and silent in the airport. She had put on the same clothes he had first seen her wearing, a tweedy skirt and sweater, and the beret with the metal insigne on it. Her shoes were low-heeled brown oxfords, good for walking, and she carried a small, anonymous overnight case. On the MATS plane flying south, Durell checked the contents of her case and found only simple cotton underthings, nothing nylon which might bring disaster to them behind the Iron Curtain.

"You won't have to worry about me," she said. "I know what to do."

He had told her briefly what he was going to try to accomplish: to find Dr. Tagy, trace McFee, and begin the investigation at the American Embassy in Vienna and the Refugee Committees for the traitor. She had listened quietly and then shook her head.

"You don't know what it is like over there, now."

"Are you afraid to go back?"

"Yes. Very much afraid. They will kill me."

"You still have your AVO contacts?"

"Yes. They are the ones who will happily see me dead, if they know I have turned traitor."

He said sharply: "You shouldn't think of yourself as a traitor. There are thousands, millions of Hungarians, who think as you do. What you are doing is for Hungary, for the freedom and dignity of your own people."

"It is only sugar-coating on the pill," she whispered.

"You don't have to come," he said. "I want your cooperation and help on a voluntary basis, Ilona. I can send you back to Washington, where you will be safe."

She looked down at her hands. "There is no safe place in the world for me, Mr. Durell."

"Sam," he suggested.

"Very well. Sam." She smiled weakly. "We will be friends?"

"I hope so."

"Miss Padgett—I heard them talking—she will be all right?"

"I think so."

"You are still in love with her, are you not?"

"Yes," Durell said.

"I am sorry for you, Sam."

The SAC plane was waiting for them at the Florida airfield, and the transfer took only ten minutes, scarcely time for Ilona to express surprise at the warmth of the sun and the palm trees bordering the field. There were only three men in the bomber crew, and they treated Durell and the girl with military reserve, young men who joked among themselves and spoke with Brooklyn and Mississippi accents. Durell and Ilona had a small storage compartment in the stern of the bomber's fusilage for themselves, equipped with bucket seats and a small folding table for writing purposes. The co-pilot brought them sandwiches and a thermos of coffee. His eyes were curious, but he knew better than to ask questions. All through the silent, high-level flight across the sea, into the gathering wings of dusk, Durell and Ilona were not interrupted.

The plane bored smoothly through the sky above the seas toward the American airbase in Spain. There was little or no feeling of motion. Time and distance had been annihilated in a shrinking world, Durell thought, and if one man died of tyranny here, it was felt all the way around the globe, because with the shrinking of distance, the responsibility of man for his fellows increased in direct proportion. No man was safe, no home was secure, as long as a portion of this small, tortured globe suffered evil. The world had changed, and was changing even more swiftly. No cry for help was too remote to be ignored, no horrid stench of totalitarian prisons could be dismissed as of no consequence to other men. The quiet backwaters of Bayou Peche Rouge, where the gum and cypress trees towered high over placid, peaceful lagoons, were no safer than the apartments in Central European cities where people cowered and whispered in dread of approaching boots. This girl beside him knew the truth, and he wished briefly that Deirdre, too, could know what he felt and how he could never abandon the task he had begun. He was only one man in a dark, shadowy war whose savagery was none the less because it was silent, where the importance of each small victory or defeat could weigh no less than the bugle-blaring battles of long ago.

He began to question the girl, probing skillfully to learn the sort of person she really was. It was not often that he took such a calculated risk, depending upon another for his own safety. Too many times he had learned the value of solitary vigilance. But he needed her, and the mission could scarcely be accomplished without her. He knew she was afraid; he wanted to know the depths of her fear, how much it had eroded from her store of brave rebellion.

"You do not have to worry about me," she said finally.

Her hands were tranquil in her lap as they sat side by side in the small compartment. "You can trust me, even though I know that death, or even worse, waits where we are going. But in a way, I am glad to go back. I am a Hungarian, and I want to help my country. Too many of us fled for reasons of personal safety, or because they were exhausted by the demands of the Communist regime, or because they saw no hope for private betterment. I have felt as if I were a coward, planning to stay in the United States. Now it is better. This is what I really wanted to do, I suppose. I want to go back and fight them, in my own country, in my own city, in the ruined streets I used to love."

"How did you ever get into the AVO, in the first place?"

She studied her strong, firm hands. "You have to know what life has been like. I am twenty-eight years old, and I never knew democracy as you know it. And I was cursed with the name of Ilona Andrassy. It is a name of nobility in Hungary, and a curse and blot on the land. We were on the fringe of that clique that resisted every improvement, every forward step of progress, since the first World War. They are the ones who backed the fascist Horthy regime and who collaborated with the Nazis when Hungary was occupied. With a name like that, when the Communists came in, it was almost impossible to survive. There was no place for an Andrassy, however dimly related we were to the real core of the family. There was no work, no place to live, nothing to do. We were not permitted to go, and we were not allowed to live where we were. I remember how it was with my father. There was nothing he could do but let himself be taken into the AVO labor battalions. They killed him there. And that, in turn, killed my mother. Only then, because I was a child who they thought would not know or remember these things, was anything done for me." She shuddered slightly. "My blood was tainted, according to their standards. They watched me as if I were some alien beast—as if a child of twelve could hurt them. But, you know, I became a good Communist. I studied Marx and Lenin and I could argue with the best of them. At first I worked in a machine factory in Csepel, the industrial district of Budapest. And they watched me. Always, there were eyes upon me. But I was a good Communist, and because I was clever and knew my Marx dialectics, I was finally permitted to attend the University of Budapest. I wanted to work on the newspaper, the *Szabad Nep*." Ilona's smile was bitter. "That means 'Free People.'"

"And the AVO?" Durell asked quietly.

"The *Allam Vedelmi Osztag*," she said. Her voice was bitter. "One had no choice. At the university, where I studied journalism, I was asked to act as an informer. You understand, the AVO used everyone, everyone. There are the controls who act as liaison groups between agents and informers and the AVO officials. They can be anyone—nightclub owners, shopkeepers, waiters. The agents are specialists who use false papers to get into factories or newspaper plants to spy on the other workers. The informers, of which I was one, used many women—housewives, workers, prostitutes, it made no difference. When they approached me to spy on my fellow students, I tried to refuse. I was told that my friends would suffer, and so I agreed. But then, when I turned in few or false reports of no harm to anyone, I was told that another member of my classes was assigned to check on me. I had no idea who it was. Life became a hell of suspicion and hatred. I tried to do as little injury to anyone as I could. There was a time when I wanted to kill myself, and they told me that if I chose suicide as a way out, my friends would be put in the labor battalions. There was no way out. None at all. They paid me, you know—they paid everyone, and forced them to sign receipts. And after a time, you begin to give up, a little bit of yourself at a time, until you are as degraded, as brutal, as callous as the others."

Durrell lit a cigarette and handed it to her. She took it without looking at him. Her face was very pale.

"After I graduated from the university, I got a job on *Szabad Nep* and I joined the Petoefi Circle—the group of writers and intellectuals who really began the October rebellion. I was still spying for the AVO. By then I knew a great deal about them—the cellar prisons, the sadistic guards. Most of the agents were scum who had also served the Horthy regime and the Gestapo during the Nazi occupation. It made no difference to the Reds. They were trained in brutality and terror, and that was all that was needed. Of course, many of the higher officials, like Bela Korvuth, were dedicated Communists, of high intelligence, well paid, living in luxury, on salaries of ten, twenty thousand forints a month, while a factory worker made eight hundred. I had no choice. I was one of them. And there was no hope for escape until October came and I saw how thousands, millions of others felt. And I was on the wrong side." She shuddered violently for a moment. "I could feel the hatred of the people for the

AVO. It was like a black, choking poison, pressing all around me. We were detested, feared.

"I was in the hall in Vaci Street when it began. I saw the massacres at the Radio Building, the ineffectuality of Nagy Imre at Parliament Square. I saw them burn down the steel statue of Stalin, and I saw the children, the children, fighting the Russian tanks, with fists, pipes, gasoline bottles, grenades strung across the streets. I heard the shouting, the yells for 'Ruszkik ki! Ruszkik ki!'—Russians, get out! I saw my city destroyed when the Mongol troops came back in the new tanks that could deflect their guns so you couldn't slip up under them to stuff gasoline rags in the air vents. I ran. I hid.

"I saw the AVO men killed, but most of us survived. I was in the crowd at Koztarsasag Square, where AVO men were hosed out of the cellar prisons—diabolical places—and torn to pieces by the people. I was hurt in the crowd, but nobody identified me then. I woke up in the Szabolcz Street Hospital, and by then it was over. The Soviet tanks had come back, shooting, bombing—oh, so bravely! Tanks, jets and machine guns against a betrayed people who had nothing but their hands to fight with. It was hopeless. There was nothing I could do. And then Major Korvuth visited me and I went back to work in the reconstituted AVO, and finally I was chosen—honored, he said—to accompany him to America for his mission."

Her mouth curved downward. Durell looked out through the small port. There was nothing to see, only black starry space, the infinite reaches of the stratosphere. No sea, no land, nothing tangible was in sight. He looked back at the girl. She was watching him with an expression of despair in her dark eyes.

"You don't believe me, do you?" she whispered. "You think I am only excusing myself for having worked with the secret police."

"I believe you," he said.

"You have heard stories like mine before. Full of excuses, pleading innocence, full of self-reproach. But mine is true."

"What will they do to you if you're caught, Ilona?"

Her face was pale. "There was a prison at Recsk. It was an extermination place. It is probably in operation again."

"You can still turn back," he said.

"Then you don't believe me?"

"I only hope you've told me the truth."

Chapter Ten

THE GIRL slept until they landed at the U.S. military airfield in western Spain. It was almost dawn here as the bomber touched down, a pale pearly light glowing in the east. The air was cold, with a bitter wind. Durell had been thinking about Deirdre, and of the finality with which she had turned away from him. He knew this distraction with thoughts other than for the mission ahead of him was dangerous, and he tried to push her image from his mind. The days ahead were dangerous enough without the added liability of risk because of carelessness. Death came quickly and greedily for the careless man in his business, and he told himself that if Deirdre did not understand him now, then nothing could be done about it and she belonged to the past. The time to think about was now, and tomorrow, and not yesterday.

In the operations office, Durell was met by a Colonel Smith, who provided him with a set of documents for himself and Ilona, arranged for by coded cable from Washington. There was time to shower and have breakfast at the airfield, in Smith's office, before a jeep was summoned and they rode for an hour to meet a plane for a commercial flight to Zurich. Veinna had been notified in advance, and a Roger Wyman, from the American Embassy, was waiting for them when they landed late in the afternoon.

Ilona had grown increasingly quiet during their eastward progress, and shortly before they landed in Austria, with the Alps glittering cold and forbidding far below their plane, she said, "One favor I would like to ask. Must we go into the city itself? There are many Hungarian refugees still in Vienna. Someone might recognize me, and that might spoil things for us before we are well started."

Durell nodded. "We'll see what Wyman says."

They used the papers given to them in Spain by Colonel Smith. He was now Janos Derosi, an engineer in the locomotive factory in Csepel, Budapest. Ilona had kept her own name and papers indicating she still worked ostensibly for *Szabad Nep*, the official Communist newspaper in Budapest.

74

Roger Wyman met them after they had gone through a routine customs inspection. He was a big blond man from Nebraska, about thirty-three, with a plainsman's face and pale blue eyes with narrow squint lines radiating from the corners. His grip was strong and hard. His position at the Embassy was that of an Undersecretary, and his manner was smooth and quick, like that of many professional Foreign Service careermen.

"You two must be starved. I've made arrangements at Victor's for dinner for the three of us. I imagine you want to be briefed about McFee. Come this way."

"We don't want to go into town," Durell said. "Ilona doesn't think it's wise, and neither do I."

"Oh?" Wyman looked at the redheaded girl with appreciation. His smile was warm, his teeth big and white. He wore a dark-green, fuzzy Habig hat, a tweedy overcoat, highly polished London cordovans. He frowned slightly. "You might be right, at that, children. Some of the Hungarians spotted an AVO man just the other day. Damned near started a riot. What do you suggest?"

"Somewhere near the border. Can you drive us, say, to Eisenstadt?"

"Sure thing. Smart move. You want to go across tonight?"

"If conditions are right," Durell said.

"It won't be easy. There's a real terror campaign going on over there, I hear. Well, come on. I've got my car outside."

It was a small Topolino, an Italian car affectionately known as a "little mouse." It was colder here than it had been at the Spanish airport. Roger Wyman's big bulk crowded the little vehicle, and his Midwestern drawl began to grate on Durell's nerves. The big man talked about his job, about the chances he'd had for advancement in the Foreign Service, about departmental politics that had kept several plums from his grasp because, as he put it, he hadn't come from some swank Boston family with drag in the right quarters. He spoke cheerfully, but under his words Durell sensed a deep resentment at the job he was in. Durel did not bring up the subject of McFee's disappearance until they were well away from the Vienna Airport, speeding eastward along a wide, concrete autobahn out of the city's suburbs.

"I took your chief to the border myself," Wyman told him. "I put him in this inn in Eisenstadt that I'm going to take you to. He wanted me to find the leak in the refugee screening apparatus we set up, and I've been working on that all day, checking dossiers on our people here. Of course, we've had to hire a great many Hungarian interpreters, and Austrians, too, and when we got orders to up the quotas, we had to work fast. Public opinion around here had us on a spot, because we weren't passing through enough refugees in comparison to other European countries. It's my feeling that in our hurry, we didn't check some of the foreign help thoroughly enough. I've been doing that all day, but so far nothing has turned up to give me a clue."

"When did you last see McFee?" Durell asked.

"At the inn, as I told you. He said he wanted to scout around for a day or so before going across the border. I advised him against trying it at all, frankly. The situation over there since the Russians came back is pretty tense. But I suggested the name of a professional guide, when he insisted, and then I had to get back to town. That was the last I saw of him."

"And he hasn't made contact since then?"

"Two nights ago. That's when I left him in Eisenstadt. Funny little chap. Not very talkative. I don't even know who or what he was after."

"You don't have to know," Durell said.

There was a faint change in Roger Wyman's broad, good-looking face. Durell wondered if it was resentment at his bluntness. Wyman said: "I tried to find the guide I recommended—Tibor Szabo. Quick youngster, full of beans. He's gone, too. I can only assume that McFee grew impatient the moment I left and took off for points east." Wyman leaned forward at the wheel of the Topolino to look at Ilona's face in the shadows. "I can recommend another guide, if you're going in after McFee."

"We won't need one," Ilona said quietly.

"You're Hungarian?"

"It doesn't matter what she is," Durell said bluntly.

There was something about Wyman that irritated him, and this didn't make sense, except that it might be an expression of his own state of nerves. He had never felt quite as tense and touchy about a job before, and there was no point in gratuitously making an enemy of the man for no good reason at all. Wyman's next words convinced him the man was only trying to be helpful.

"If you're going across after McFee, I can tell you something about Tibor Szabo's usual route. He went by way of Györ—that's about sixty miles from Budapest—and usually holed up at a farm in the outskirts of that town. Run by an uncle of Tibor's, Geza Hegedus. Tibor had quite a system. Chances are if your McFee went across with him, they stopped at Hebedus's farm for the rest of the night."

Durell looked at Ilona, and she nodded slightly, indicating that she was familiar with the route. He felt the warm pressure of her body against him as they sat squeezed together in the little car, and he was suddenly impatient to keep going, to be rid of Wyman as soon as possible and get on with the job. There was no reason, actually, to assume that Dickinson McFee had met with personal disaster, despite the desperate risk of probing into Budapest these days. McFee might have decided not to check back until he found some definite trace of Dr. Tagy in the ruined city; or his line of communication may have broken down somewhere. Durell began to feel more optimistic. Ilona's gloved hand crept into his and he squeezed her fingers lightly against the slight nervous trembling he felt in her. They had arrived here in good time. Even granted that Bela Korvuth, back in the States, got wind of Tagy's presence here in Hungary, it would take Korvuth days to double back on the physicist's trail. By that time, Durell hoped, their swift probe behind the Iron Curtain would be successfully finished.

It was eleven o'clock when they arrived in the small town of Eisenstadt. Durell felt no sense of weariness, despite the vast distance they had traveled since noon in Washington that day. His sense of time had become slightly distorted by their race eastward, into the night, away from Washington's Sunday calm. His wounded arm felt cramped and stiff from being crowded in Wyman's little car, but it was not enough to trouble him seriously. He was more concerned about Ilona's growing tension as they neared the border. It was not easy for her to go back into a terror she knew so intimately.

The inn Wyman took them to in Eisenstadt was small and unobtrusive, and Wyman, in poor German, ordered a late supper for them. Durell did not object as Wyman cheerfully went on to arrange for two rooms for their use that night. The place was not crowded. The dining room was rustic, dimly lighted, and they were the only occupants at the tables, although a small bar across the common room was noisy with several men in rough clothing, drinking beer. Except for the first curious glances at them, nobody paid much attention. Durell tried to spot anybody who might have a more than usual interest in a couple who looked like

Hungarians in the company of an obvious American like Wyman, but he didn't see anything to alert him and he relaxed gratefully over the hot food served by a plump and cheerful hausfrau.

For some minutes he probed Wyman about McFee, looking for anything that might yield a hint of trouble for the little man; but Wyman's impression of McFee was mostly negative, even resentful of the way McFee had shut him out of information. Durell got Wyman to talk about himself, mainly to set Ilona at ease, and Wyman was not averse to yielding his history as a Nebraska farmboy, a football star, a scholarship man whose ambitions in the Foreign Service had come up against the grueling reality of bureaucracy and frustration. Yet the man seemed competent and able, efficient in the manner he sketched in his preliminary efforts to probe the screening personnel for anything suspicious.

"Will you be taking off tonight?" Wyman asked finally.

"I haven't decided yet. Ilona is rather tired."

"You both look a little beat. After all, another night shouldn't crack too many eggs. Is something wrong with your arm, Durell?" he asked suddenly.

Durell felt a swift rise of alarm and anger. His voice was quietly savage. "You know what my name is here."

"Oh, sure. Sorry. But this place is safe as a church. Nothing to worry about. But you're holding your arm as if it troubles you."

"It does," Durell said. "I got a bullet in it recently."

Wyman looked flustered under Durell's steady, dark stare. "You don't have to get sore. It was just a slip. Nobody heard us."

"I think you'd better take off," Durell said.

"Well, all right. I'm really sorry." Wyman stood up, smiling. There was a burst of heavy laughter from the bar, but the backs of the men there were all turned toward them. "If you'd like, I'll leave my car. There's a bus back to Vienna at midnight. If there's anything I can do—by the way, you have your money changed to forints, haven't you?"

"Yes," Durell said. There had been a packet of thick Hungarian currency among the papers Colonel Smith gave him at the Spanish airport. "We'll take the car, with thanks. I'm sorry I snapped. It's a touchy business."

"My fault, entirely." Wyman looked grateful as Durell relaxed. "I'm always talking too much. Big fault. Not the sort of thing a man in the Foreign Service should have on

his record. I guess it's just that you people intrigue me—
I often wish I were in your branch, instead of doing the
routine paperwork they give me." He flushed and broke off
again. "There I go once more. I'd better leave before you
think I'm a complete ass."

He went out quickly, waving to the fat waitress who
brought Durell and Ilona their coffee. Durell watched the
big blond man out of sight, and he was silent until the
waitress left the vicinity of their table. He saw that Ilona
was very pale again.

"A few more minutes with that man," she said, "and we
might as well have worn some signs around our necks."

"Take it easy," he told her. "You're too keyed up."

"I can't help it. I didn't like Mr. Wyman."

"Are you nervous about staying here tonight?"

"I think the sooner we move on, the better."

"We can use Wyman's car to get near the border, anyway.
Do you know the road?"

"Quite well. It will not be easy."

Durell looked at the fine bones of her face, the softness
of her mouth when she smiled, even though the smile was
forced. He touched her hand.

"None of it will be easy. Let's go."

Chapter Eleven

A THIN, cold mist lay along the swamps of the border. The
night was white and frozen, with hoarfrost on the brittle
reeds and the still, bare branches of clumps of birch trees.
The ground felt like iron, frozen underfoot. Durell ran the
Topolino into a barn a mile from the boundary and hoped it
would still be there when they returned—if they were lucky,
and if they returned. From the barn, they walked along a
progressively deteriorating lane, picking their way by means
of the cold blue starshine that gave an unearthly aspect to
the landscape. Somewhere far off a dog barked and barked.
To the south, across the rolling fields of Burgenland, a spotlight suddenly shot straight up, probing the sky, and then
swept down in a leveling arc and blinked out. Durell walked
along with the girl in silence. She seemed familiar enough

with the road. It was past midnight, and nothing living stirred in the frozen white stillness around them.

"We are almost there," Ilona said, halting. "See, you can make out the banks of the canal—that wall of earth there. It is in Hungary. About a quarter of a mile to the north, you will see the wooden watchtower."

"Is it manned?"

"With the new R Troops—the old AVO personnel. And probably the Russians, set to watch the AVO. Two miles beyond the canal, if we get through the marshes, there is a rather good road and some farms where we might be able to borrow a cart or a truck. But the swamps ahead are difficult."

The girl's voice was quiet and firm now. Now that they were on the move, she seemed to have lost some of the tension that had possessed her earlier. In the starlight, her face was calm, her glance objective. Durell looked toward the watch tower. For a moment he could not define it, then it came clearly through the white mists that gave the night a strange luminosity. There was no sign of movement in the tower, and he could not tell if it were occupied. Ilona made a sign with her hand and they moved forward toward the bank of the canal.

It was little more than a wide ditch at this point, and the temperature fortunately had frozen the surface. Durell tested the ice with his weight, then walked quickly across, with Ilona behind him. The marshes below the canal embankment stretched in every direction, seemingly limitless, with reeds clashing softly, taller than his head. He had heard how some refugees, fleeing from the return of the Russian terror, had wandered lost, for days, without a guide. But Ilona moved forward with confidence, every aspect of her changed. She turned left, slid down the canal embankment, and indicated a footpath that was swallowed up by the reeds ahead. Durell nodded and signaled her to lead the way.

The strange white night was perilous in its silence. Now and then Ilona paused and they listened. From far away came a faint, rapid thudding noise, and he knew a machine gun was being fired.

"A Russian guitar," Ilona whispered. "We will have to be on the watch for patrol dogs."

There was nothing to see. The footing was uncertain and treacherous as the path meandered from hummock to hummock in the frozen swamps. Now and then a breeze stirred and the reeds clashed and rattled in brittle reply. But if the marsh reeds cut off his vision, it served equally well to screen them from the eyes of the border patrol. They went about a quarter of a mile and rested for a few moments.

"A road begins up ahead. We will have to cross it," Ilona whispered. "I think you had better be ready for trouble."

Durell took his gun out. It felt clumsy in his gloved hand, and he pulled the glove off with his teeth and held the gun in his bare fingers, feeling the quick bite of the cold.

"After you."

An opening appeared in the reeds ahead. Mist moved in thin, tenuous streamers over a graveled road, and from a distance not far off, Durell heard the sudden sound of a car or truck engine starting up. He could see the watch tower now, a gaunt, spidery structure of heavy timbers, topped with a machine-gun platform, two spotlights, and a small enclosure with glass windows. Directly ahead, on the other side of the road, was a heavy fence of barbed wire. He knew that this would be their most formidable barrier. He could not tell if it were electrified, and he was not equipped with wire cutters. They would have to get through the best way they could.

Ilona waved him on ahead and he crossed the road in a low crouch and dropped in the dark shadows near the wire fence. Looking back, he saw the girl rise, ready to run after him. There was no warning when the star shell was fired. One moment there was only the eerie white frost of the night. The next, with a slight popping sound, a signal shell burst overhead and shed a dazzling radiance over the swamp, the road and the watch tower.

He stood in stark brilliance with Ilona against the wire fence.

There was no chance to escape. A man shouted from Durell's right, and he spun quickly, saw the dimly running shape and the lift of the man's arms and the glint of the short-barreled automatic weapon. He threw Ilona to the ground as the gun began to chatter. A shallow ditch ran along the side of the road and he followed the girl's rolling body into it as the slugs kicked up frozen chips of sod where they had been standing. There was only the one burst, and then silence. High overhead, the star shell fell slowly, its unnnatural brightness beginning to fade.

"Are you hit?" Durell whispered.

"No. But it is all over."

The star shell went out. The strange whiteness of the night seemed darker now, and Durell slid away from the girl, on

hands and knees, keeping below the lip of the ditch. Footsteps crunched on the gravel roadway nearby, pausing cautiously, then moving nearer again. He lay still, his gun in his
hand. From the watch tower came the dim shrilling of a
whistle, and there was a muttered curse from the border
guard easing toward the barbed-wire fence. Durell began to
hope that the man was not sure of what he had fired at.
Perhaps they had not been identified as anything more than
suspicious shadows, and nerves had triggered the guard's finger.
A dog barked in irritated, repetitive bursts of nervous sound.
Durell waited. The guard's booted footsteps were very near
now. They paused, and Durell came up fast, the gun in his
hand as he scrambled up from the ditch. Luck was on his side.
The guard's back was toward him, his great-coated figure
formless in the darkness. He wore a fur shako against the
bitter cold, and Durell slashed at the base of his skull with
the gun. There was no error in the precision of his blow.
The guard stumbled forward, dropped his automatic rifle,
and sprawled on his face in the middle of the road. Durell
picked up the man's gun and ran back toward Ilona.

"Come on. He'll be out for a few minutes."

Her face was pale and ghostly. "Are you all right?"

"Yes. Hurry."

The barbed-wire fence had been put up hurriedy since the
return of the Russian troops to the frontier. Durell moved
along it until he found a reasonably fair gap in the strands,
tramped on one to push it down, and helped the girl slide
through. In a moment he followed. They didn't look back
as they ran on through the swamps, heading eastward.

Afterward, when Durell thought about it, he knew he could
not have made his way successfully without the girl. She did
not lose her sense of direction for a moment. Twenty minutes of alternate trotting and walking brought them out of
the swamp into rolling fields. The highway was where she
said it would be. The farm she picked, with its peasant house
and warm barn, smelling of hay and cattle, was exactly as she
had promised. There was a small gray Skoda parked behind
the barn. Ilona told Durell to stay in the shadows and walked
around the back of the farmhouse. No light came on in the
place, but he knew she had knocked and spoken to someone
and gone in. She was not absent long. In a few minutes she
came running back, carrying a paper sack and the car keys.

"It's all right. I have some bread and cheese. We are to

leave the car at the farm of Tibor's uncle in Györ. Can you drive a Skoda?"

Durell nodded. "Didn't they ask any questions?"

"I told them I was Tibor's woman." In the darkness, Durell saw her smile of wry amusement. "I also said I was helping Tibor in his work as a guide. Business has fallen off lately, since a division of Mongolian troops have occupied the frontier area."

"Did you ask about McFee?"

"He came through with Tibor Szabo last night."

Durell threw the Russian automatic rifle into the hay loft before they left, and put his own gun on the floor of the car between his feet. The distance to Györ was less than an hour's run. The countryside changed from the low marshland along the frontier to rolling hills and fertile plains, scrupulously farmed by the tight-fisted Magyar peasants. They met no traffic on the road for the first part of the run, and when they saw a long line of headlights moving up ahead, Durell pulled off the road into thick brush to let a convoy thunder past. They were T-54 Soviet tanks, low-slung, swift, with sloping, heavily armored sides and semi-automatic cannon. Some of the hatches of the squad leaders were open, and Durell saw the helmeted machine-gunners, their faces dark and anonymous in the starlight. The convoy seemed to go on forever, thunderous and arrogant, and Durell counted over two hundred of the T-54's before the tail end of the procession roared by with two Russian-made jeeps.

"The conquerors," Ilona murmured. Her voice was thin. "How I hate them!"

It was almost three o'clock in the morning when they turned into the frozen mud road to the farm of Geza Hegedus, in the outskirts of industrial Györ. The place was low and rambling, built of stone for the most part, with tidy barns and outbuildings. The city lay in dark slumber only a few miles beyond. Geza Hegedus was a small, wiry man with dark hair and the intense, acute face of the Magyar peasant. He appeared at the back door of the farm in a battered Army overcoat and boots, his thick gray hair awry, his heavy mustache scraggly over a worried mouth.

"Please, do not make any noise, my friends." Durell's knowledge of Hungarian was just enough to permit him to get the gist of the man's whispered words. "You are heading for Austria?"

"We are going back to Budapest for more people," Ilona told him. "Have you a place for us to sleep tonight?"

"You have papers?"

"They are satisfactory," Ilona said. "We were hoping to find your nephew Tibor here."

"He is gone. I don't know when I shall see the fool again." The farmer looked at Durell. "Doesn't this one speak at all?"

"He prefers silence, old man," Ilona said. "You do not see him. You will not remember him. Do you understand?"

"You are all crazy. Crazy! The frontiers are sealed tighter than ever, and yet you go on. Fools and cowards run away, pay you to take them to the West. What will happen to Hungary if our people all run away? It was not like this in the old days."

"We need no lectures from you, only a room for the night. And silence. We will pay you well."

"I take no money for my services," the peasant grumbled. He held the door of the farmhouse open, his manner grudging. "You have hidden your car?"

"In the barn."

"Come in, then. It is cold tonight."

The kitchen had a stone floor and a huge Russian-type stove in one corner, a massive oak table and equally heavy, worn chairs. Hegedus drew thick curtains over the windows and lit a kerosene lamp. His eyes returned worriedly to Durell's tall, silent figure.

"I do not trust this one. He looks like a foreigner."

"He is," Ilona said. "He searches for the man Tibor brought here last night."

Hegedus scowled. "Tibor is a fool. This man is worse, if he hopes for success. I kept warning Tibor, over and over again, that this business was too risky now. It was good enough in the first days, when the frontier was open and the AVO was in hiding. But they are all back now, all of them, and worse than ever. Every day I live in fear that they will find the guests Tibor brings me."

"Where is Tibor now?"

"I don't know."

"And the man Tibor was taking to Budapest?"

Hegedus grunted. "He is probably praying for death."

Durell felt a small chill of apprehension at the farmer's manner. He spoke to Ilona. "Ask him what he means. Ask if anything happened."

Hegedus looked up sharply at the sound of Durell's English.

His manner changed. Suspicion flared in his sharp, peasant's eyes, and then was replaced by fear. "I do not like this one here. The one Tibor brought also spoke English. And it was disastrous. Every moment now, I expect the AVO to be back with more questions."

"What happened?" Ilona asked sharply. "Were they caught?"

"Tibor escaped. The little man was taken prisoner. Last night, Tibor and the little man stayed here only for a bite of food before going on toward the city. But they did not get far. Tibor pushed his luck like a wild man. I've been warning him that the police were suspicious. They were waiting on the road, about a mile from here. The little man was taken, but Tibor escaped."

"Did you see it happen?"

"My neighbors saw it. It is as I said. Tibor's friend was captured. Tibor escaped into the woods. He is finished now. They will hunt him like a wild animal, and he will be killed."

"And the foreigner?"

Hegedus shrugged. "Who knows what the AVO does to him this minute?" The old man drew a deep breath. "I do not want you here. It is too dangerous. But it will also be dangerous if you move on now. I have only one room to spare, upstairs, in the attic. You will have to stay together, and for the love of God, make no sound, no matter what you may hear down in these rooms. Do you understand?"

Ilona turned to Durell. "Did you get what he said? McFee is caught." Her eyes were somber. "Do you want to go on?"

Durell saw the shadows of fatigue under her eyes. Outside, the night had turned inky dark in the hours before dawn. They would be too conspicuous traveling in the Skoda now, and he knew the girl had pushed herself to the limit of her endurance.

"We'll stay here and get a few hours of sleep," he decided.

The attic room that Hegedus showed them to was small and barren and icy cold, with hoarfrost gleaming white and icy on the roughhewn rafters. There was no bed or furniture of any kind except a crude straw mattress in one corner, with two blankets rumpled upon it. A small gable window, partly covered with frost, opened on a shed roof six feet below. Hegedus exchanged a few more words with Ilona, and then closed the batten door and his booted footsteps faded on the crude ladder down to the main floor of the farmhouse. There were no other sounds in the place. Durell prowled the tiny room uneasily. It had the feeling of a trap. He tried the door, wondering if the old man had bolted it slyly on the outside, but it opened readily and he looked down the ladder into empty darkness. There was a bolt on the inside, however, and he threw it when he closed the door again.

Ilona stood uncertainly near the mattress in the corner. The farmer had left them his kerosene lamp, and her face looked wan in the pale yellow glow. Durell took his gun from his pocket and put it on the floor beside the blankets and then turned down the wick on the lamp. Darkness folded around them, relieved only by the faint glow of light from the city of Györ a few miles to the east.

Ilona spoke in the darkness, her voice uncertain. "Should we stay here, do you think?"

"You need the rest. A few hours of sleep will help."

"But your friend is in the hands of the AVO—"

"There is nothing we can do for McFee right now," Durell said. He moved through the darkness to her dim figure and told her to sit down and cover up with the blankets. The cold in the room seemed more penetrating than the icy air outside. He felt a shiver move through him and he knew he, too, was more tired than he had wanted to admit. "Do you think Hegedus can be trusted?"

"I don't know," she whispered. "I don't like this place."

He did not want to tell her of his own uneasiness. He heard a strange, faint noise, and he knew her teeth were chattering in the cold darkness, and he drew her gently down onto the straw mattress and pulled the rough blankets over them. Instantly she burrowed against him, her body movements like that of a small animal. With his arms around her, her control gave way and she shuddered violently, her breath coming quick and warm and irregularly against his cheek.

"I'm afraid," she whispered. "And you—you are disappointed in me."

"No, it isn't that."

"You are silent, though. You are thinking of something else."

"There's a job ahead of us."

"No, it isn't that. It is—something—someone else."

He thought of Deirdre. "Yes."

"You have lost her? The girl Bela Korvuth shot?"

"I think so."

"She would not see you at the hospital?"

"I almost wish she hadn't," Durell said.

She was silent for a moment, then whispered: "I am sorry. Sorry for you and for her. She is foolish. A woman who had your love would be a very lucky woman, I think. If she does not understand what made you risk her life to get Bela Korvuth, then she is stupid, too. I am sorry to talk like this about her, but I have thought of this Deirdre woman, too. If you loved me, there would be nothing you could do that I would consider to be wrong. That is the way love should be."

"Perhaps. I'd rather not talk about it."

"You should," she whispered fiercely. Her arms were tight around him and she burrowed closer against his body under the blankets. "It is necessary to talk about it. You are unhappy and you think about her all the time, instead of thinking of what we must do here. You know as well as I how dangerous this can be. You may grow careless, or absent, and in one moment, we can both be destroyed."

He felt warmer now, under the blankets, with the girl twined close to him. He knew that she was right. He had been thinking of Deirdre too much, he had allowed her to haunt his mind when nothing but the mission ahead of them should have occupied his thoughts. They had been lucky so far. But tomorrow, or the next day, or perhaps in the next hour, death could come very easily to both of them.

"She has rejected you," Ilona whispered. "Why should you care about her now? If she refuses to understand, you must forget her. A man like you must be complete, always, at all times. Not torn apart by a foolish woman's whims."

He knew of no answer for her. Her dark hair was soft and perfumed against his face, and he was aware that the closeness of her body was no longer in demand for warmth, but for something more. The imperative, animal movements she now made against him were plain and obvious in their intent. Why not? he thought. There was nothing but bitterness and rejection behind him. The past was dead. He was alive, here and now, in this lonely alien place. The odds for continuing to stay alive were heavily stacked against him. For this brief time, in this small, dark place, there was a moment's peace, a brief warmth, an offer to give and a demand to receive. He felt Ilona's arms tighten about him, and then she suddenly released him and he knew by her movements that she was taking off her heavy winter clothing under the protecting warmth of the blankets they shared.

"Sam?" she whispered.

There was no need to reply. He felt a responsive stirring within him, as if something that had recently been lost was now found again, springing to new life and hope. He did not love Ilona, and she knew it. Yet in their mutual loneliness and in the danger they shared, perhaps they were closer in needing one another than others in warm safety might be. His pulse quickened as she turned back toward him, and then there was the silk of her body pressing against him, stirring and waking him, until he took her back into his arms. Her lips pressed with avid hunger against his.

"Do not think of yesterday or tomorrow," she whispered. "Yesterday is gone and done with; and tomorrow may never be. We are here, and it is now, and we owe each other nothing but our lives."

He kissed her gently, and then, feeling her quick, impatient movement against him, he took her in the cold, dark stillness of the attic room.

Chapter Twelve

For an hour or more afterward, Durell lay quietly with the girl asleep in his arms. He was not sure later whether or not he slept, too. He was aware of her weight against him, of the warmth and sweetness of her breath against his cheek. She sleeps like a child, he thought, safe and warm, and at peace after having been frightened. He felt a deep sense of gratitude toward her, even knowing that her giving of herself had been a deliberate act, designed to help him and clear away the deep-rooted uncertainties that had shrouded him. Perhaps in a way she had simply been selfish, concerned with her own safety that depended in as many ways upon his strength in this situation as he, in turn, depended on her. Yet her giving had been frank and uncomplicated, an expression of her desperate need for life and warmth. No promises were made and none had been demanded. She slept, trusting him. And he lay awake, listening to the sounds of the night.

There was only the faintest lightening of the night sky through the tiny attic window now. It would soon be dawn. The farmhouse was quiet, although now and then there came a faint creaking of timbers as wood and nails reacted to the intense outer cold. From far away came the high, thin piping of a train whistle, and he remembered the sounds of trains in the night when he had been a boy in Bayou Peche Rouge, when the harsh horns of the diesels had sent his imagination vaulting to the far corners of the world. There were not many places in the world now that were strange to him. Yet as a man he had learned that one place was very much like another, this farm like that, this city like the others, this nation like its neighbor. It came down, in essence, to people everywhere, to the desperate, universal hunger throughout the tormented world for peace and dignity and freedom. And it was because of this, Durell knew, that he could never quit or turn aside from the job assigned to him. He would go on working and fighting and doing what had to be done as long as he was able, as long as he lived. And it was this feeling in him, this deep and tender sympathy for all men everywhere, hidden under the hard, highly trained exterior of his working personality, that he could never convey to Deirdre or anyone. This girl beside him understood how he felt. No words were necessary. He would never consciously admit what might be considered softness or idealism, since his opponents in the dark war in which he fought were neither soft nor given to any ideals except the lusts for personal power, modern Caesars bestriding a world that now, for the first time since time itself began, could be destroyed by the touch of an idiot's grasping fingers.

He did not know exactly when he became uneasy. Perhaps it was with his growing awareness of soft, subtle sounds throughout the house. Not all of them came from below the attic room, either. The cold, still dawn was still half an hour away, but a faint, amorphous light now outlined the gable window, and the still air seemed to ring silently with the cold. He sat up, sliding away from Ilona's weight, and picked up his gun.

The girl was instantly, quietly awake.

"What is it?" she whispered.

"I'm not sure. I thought I heard something."

"Shall I get dressed?"

"Yes."

He stood up now, the gun in his hand, feeling the cold bite of stagnant attic air as he pushed the blankets aside. The girl dressed in haste under the protection of the covers over their improvised bed. The hours just past were forgotten.

He moved with care over the floor boards toward the door.

A low murmur of voices, just faintly discernible, touched his straining senses. Gently, a fraction at a time, he slid the bolt free and opened the door and looked down the crude ladder that led to a room just off the kitchen. A protesting, thin voice speaking in quick tones of alarm was answered by a growled command in Russian. Durell turned as a small sound came from Ilona.

"There are men outside. Two of them. A Russian and an AVO." Her mouth formed the words that were almost inaudible. Durell nodded and closed the door and bolted it again. His pulse began to hammer and he waited a moment, resisting the panicky feeling of pressure, of a trap closing around him. His uneasy hunch about this place had been right.

He moved silently to the window and exerted controlled strength against the sash. Apparently it had been used recently, and it opened inward without sound. An icy wind blew into the attic room. Below, the slightly slanting shed roof he had noticed before was white with frost. He could see a corner of the Hegedus barn, the dim gleam of headlights from a car that had approached in disconcerting silence. The crunch of a boot made him draw back a bit. A uniformed man walked by, pacing with the meticulous solemnity of bored sentries everywhere.

He turned and saw Ilona standing beside him. He did not understand the expression on her face. From downstairs came the sudden crash of breaking furniture, a man's shout, the sound of a blow, a sudden shrill scream of pain.

"It is Geza Hegedus," Ilona whispered. "They are asking him about you."

Durell's face was suddenly blank. "About me?"

"About an American they know is hiding somewhere near here."

"How could they know about that?"

Ilona said in a flat, dead voice: "We are destroyed. We have been betrayed."

The sound of another blow, another scream came from below. Durell looked through the small window again. The pacing guard was out of sight. He drew a deep, steadying breath. There was no time to consider the implications of Ilona Andrassy's words. He nodded, took the girl's arm, and told her to get out on the shed roof below. She obeyed quickly, without question, her body agile as she slid over the sill, clung for a moment to the casing, and then dropped the foot or so to the glistening, frosty shingles beneath. For an instant Durell's heart seemed to stop as her foot slipped and she started to fall toward the edge of the shed roof. But she caught herself, balancing precariously, and a moment later he followed and joined her.

The sound of the guard's booted feet came from around the corner of the farmhouse. Durell slid down to the edge of the roof and waited. The man appeared in a moment. Durell jumped. Both feet struck the man in the small of his back and he went forward, catapulted to his knees, the automatic rifle spurting from his gloved hands. Before the guard could do more than grunt, Durell had recovered, whirled, and chopped with his gun at the nape of the guard's neck. The man fell forward, sprawling on the dark, frozen ground, and Durell straightened. His arm ached and he felt under his coat at the bandages over the bullet wound in his shoulder. They seemed secure. The jolt of his drop had not started it bleeding again. He looked up as Ilona came down to the edge of the shed roof and jumped after him.

"Let's go," he whispered.

They ran through the icy dawn toward the Skoda hidden in the barn. Durell did not like to think of what was happening to Geza Hegedus, inside the farmhouse. There was no alarm as he hauled the barn doors open and scrambled into the car with the girl. Evidently the men inside the farmhouse were busy tormenting the old farmer.

Their luck held until he got the car backed out of the barn and heading for the road. Then he heard a dim, faint shout from the house, and an instant later a shot crashed and a bullet smashed the rear window of the little Skoda. Durell tramped on the gas pedal. The road was slippery with dawn ice, and the wheels spun and they skidded sidewise onto the highway. Another shot smashed after them, ricocheting off the bonnet. Durell looked back and saw three men running toward the large dark sedan parked in front of Hegedus's house. He cursed softly, wondering why he had slipped up by not disabling the car before getting out the Skoda. It was panic, and the surprise of the trap, that had made him run too fast. He yanked the wheel left and the little Skoda's tires bit on the highway surface and they straightened up, rocking perilously, headed for Györ. Ilona looked backward.

"They're coming now. Drive faster."

The road twisted downward through a thick grove of woodland where the gray dawn light had not penetrated. Durell pushed the little car to the limits of its speed. There was no traffic, and no roadblocks were in sight as they soon began flashing past sleeping houses and a factory or two in the outskirts of the industrial town. The pursuing car was a quarter of a mile behind, hidden from sight now and then by the twists of the road. They flashed over a bridge, and Durell suddenly braked, yanking the Skoda around a tight corner and across a railroad siding where signal lights blinked a wan orange-red. A freight train was coming toward the massive pile of brick factory nearby. He looked back through the rear-vision mirror and did not see the pursuing sedan, and took his foot off the gas pedal. Up ahead was a yellow trolley not unlike those that had been used in New York City until recent years. It was crowded with laborers, and he looked at his watch, saw it was almost six o'clock, and knew the city was coming awake. He drove more slowly, knowing that any car was conspicuous in this city, usually considered official by the passers-by who saw it coming. He turned the next corner and the next. The street became rough and pitted with chuck holes, narrow and wet between the grim walls of industrial plants. Behind them, the freight train whistled and he heard the clashing of couplings as the train slowed on the siding.

"We'd better ditch this," he said to the girl.

"We're still a long way from Budapest."

"Would it be safe to take a train?"

"If we moved quickly."

Neither was ready to discuss what was uppermost in their minds. The girl looked tense and frightened as he stopped the car near a high iron gateway between two manufacturing plants and they got out. She said, "This way. It's over a mile to the railroad station."

They walked through the brightening dawn, along streets that were coming alive sullenly with workingmen and women. Here and there Durell saw torn-up asphalt and the marks of tank treads and the occasional pocked façade of a building that had been sprayed by machine-gun bullets in the October uprising. He remembered there had been considerable fighting in this city, too, although Györ had suffered lightly in comparison to Budapest. Durell walked neither too fast nor too slow, and Ilona kept up with his stride. It was bright daylight when they reached the railroad station, and Durell walked through the dingy waiting room looking for danger in the form of police, and saw only the uniformed guards he had expected. There were several dozen people, huddled in clumsy overcoats, waiting on the hard wooden benches. There was no sign of unusual danger, and he began to hope that the men in the sedan were still of the opinion that he and Ilona were still with the Skoda. His mind cast ahead as well as backward, and he sent Ilona to buy their tickets with a handful of forints he gave her. When she came back with the tickets she told him there was a half-hour wait before the train departed for Budapest. A small coffee shop in one end of the station seemed to be the best place to wait. It was fairly crowded, and they could make themselves anonymous among the other waiting passengers in case the station building was checked before train time.

Ilona ordered coffee and a roll, and he nodded to the waiter to duplicate the order for himself. Ilona's hand trembled slightly as she lit a cigarette.

"I feel exposed. This is not the best place for us to be."

"It's our only chance of getting to Budapest," Durell told her. "Speak quietly. My Hungarian is too obviously foreign." There were three men and a woman at the next round table, in the coffee shop, but except for the first casual glances sent their way as they sat down, nobody paid them any attention. "Do you know of any other way we can get there?"

"They may think you are Russian," Ilona said. "It will be all right. I'm just nervous, that's all. A little shaken up."

"Who did it?" Durell asked. "Who tipped off the secret police that an American was hiding at Hegedus's farm?"

"I wish I knew," she murmured. "I'm frightened by it."

"Could it have been Tibor Szabo?"

"How could he have known you would follow so soon?"

"That's right," Durell said. "Not even McFee knew I was coming in after him. Even if Hegedus's was betrayed, say, by Tibor—if Tibor has been captured—they wouldn't be looking for me there last night, would they?"

"We don't know that Tibor has been caught. But McFee—perhaps he has talked."

"He hasn't," Durell said flatly. "He wouldn't."

"You are very sure of your man," the redheaded girl said.

"Yes. McFee is the one element I am sure of."

She looked down at her cup of coffee. She had taken only one sip of it. "You are not sure of me, Sam?"

"I don't know how you could have tipped off the police we were here. And you could have stopped me when we got out of that damned attic room."

She flushed slightly. "Thank you. Thank you for your trust."

"I'm just trying to look at it from every direction."

"It will go worse for me, if I am caught, than for you."

"We'll both die," Durell said. "That's true."

"But they will see to it that I die slowly," Ilona said.

One of the men at the next table was staring at her. Durell reached forward and patted her hand and smiled. "Drink your coffee, darling."

"I don't want it."

"It will do you good. It's a cold morning."

"All right."

The man at the next table looked away and resumed his conversation with the other two men and the stout woman with them. It was not very warm in the coffee shop, and the station was inadequately heated, and everyone at the tables wore their overcoats and hats. It was remarkably quiet in contrast to the subdued, constant waves and echoes of sound in an American railroad station, Durell thought. It was the quiet of sullen, despairing terror, of a people afraid to laugh and talk. Durell broke his roll and ate it and finished his coffee. Ilona drank her coffee slowly, her dark brown eyes reflecting angry, golden glints.

"How can you suspect me after last night?" she asked angrily. "Do you regret anything?"

"Of course not."

"It was nothing. You owe me nothing, I owe you nothing, for last night. You must not make anything out of it. We needed each other and we were good for each other, were we not?"

"I'm still thinking of who betrayed us," Durell said.

Her fingers moved nervously over the porcelain table top. "I think you know," she whispered. "I think we both know. I'm sorry I mentioned the other thing. I didn't intend to. I'm afraid, that's all."

"So am I," he said. "Maybe it's a good thing."

"Please forgive me. I just don't want you to suspect me, that's all. We must trust each other. Our lives depend on it."

"I know that. Are you thinking of Roger Wyman?"

"Yes," she said. "He is the only one who knew our route, and who knew where we would stop to rest."

He nodded. "Roger Wyman."

It was there and he could not deny it, as much as he hated to think about it. Truth had an ugly face sometimes. All treachery and betrayal was ugly. But Dickinson McFee had been betrayed night before last, a few minutes after leaving Geza Hegedus's farm. He had been caught by the secret police a mile from the farm. Yet Tibor Szabo had escaped somehow, if the old farmer's word could be trusted. Maybe it was Tibor. But he didn't believe it, even though he had never met the young freedom fighter who had found a way to fight by guiding people to safety over the frontier. And it was difficult to believe that his uncle, Geza Hegedus, had betrayed him, too. He knew that one of the strongest Magyar traits was the intense feeling of family solidarity. It was not likely that Hegedus had betrayed his nephew. Or McFee. It could not be discounted completely, but his mind kept turning back to Roger Wyman. If a traitor explained the influx of a Red apparatus among the refugees admitted to the United States, Wyman was in a perfect position to organize it through the screening personnel. McFee had contacted only Wyman, and McFee had been arrested, caught almost as soon as he had crossed the frontier. And the same thing would have been his own fate, except for a bit of luck.

He suddenly remembered that Geza Hegedus had volunteered the information that McFee had been caught and arrested. Would Hegedus have offered that knowledge, knowing it would alert Durell, if he planned to call in the secret police an hour or two later? Not likely. Hegedus could be eliminated, so it left no one else but Wyman. The big Nebraska farm boy, frustrated career diplomat, big and handsome and flat broke, aware of talents in himself, perhaps, that were not recognized, that were lost in the sluggish bureaucracy in which he had tried to carve a career for himself. There was no one else.

Ilona said: "Please, darling. Don't look at me like that."

He had not been aware that he was staring at her. "I'm sorry. I was thinking of Roger Wyman."

"It is not easy to accept the knowledge of a traitor," she said.

"Wyman knows that McFee isn't an ordinary agent. He knows that McFee would come here only on something of top priority. He'll put two and two together, and come up with Dr. Tagy. And that means Bela Korvuth, back in the States, will be informed. Bela will come streaking back as fast as he can make it. It cuts down our time considerably."

"Should we go back after Wyman?" Ilona asked.

"No. He can wait."

"He will make things even more dangerous for us."

"It can't be helped."

There was an announcement over the loud-speaker in the waiting room, and Ilona nodded and they stood up. Durell paid the waiter with his forints and they moved toward the Budapest train. Nobody stopped them.

Chapter Thirteen

BUDAPEST still carried all the scars of bitter fighting and destruction in the bright winter sunlight. From the station in Buda, on the west bank of the Danube that flowed north and south through the twin city, Durell and Ilona walked across Parliament Square, where much of the heaviest fighting and slaughter had taken place. The big, ornate neo-Gothic Parliament building, with its gray walls and balconies, looked busy and normal except for shell and bullet scars. A gang of laborers was repairing the paving where tank treads and grenades had torn up the street. There were a great many blue-uniformed police everywhere. The populace looked sullen, hurrying about their morning tasks, with little conversation and no laughter. It was a city scarred by destruction, condemned to terror. Soviet troops still patrolled the sidewalks, and Durell did not miss the alien, Mongolian cast to their features. Their voices were loud and arrogant—the harsh assurance of the conquerors. From Parliament Square they walked three kilometers to the Radio Building, where the first serious fighting had begun back in October. Here the destruction of shot and shell was more in evidence. The purpose of his walk was not aimless. He wanted to be sure there was no one on their trail, and he took his time about it, strolling quietly with Ilona, doubling back around the block now and then or pausing to watch the reflections of the street in shop windows. They seemed safe enough.

Ilona talked brightly all the while they walked, clinging to Durell's arm as if they were lovers with no thought or consequence to their surroundings. Yet he knew her dark brown eyes missed none of the faces they passed, and once when he turned a corner and started walking right her fingers tightened convulsively on his arm.

"Not this way, darling," she smiled. "AVO headquarters are just down the street. Someone might recognize me and wonder what I'm doing here when I'm supposed to be overseas."

They turned and walked the other way. On the train they had decided on a course of action if their arrival in Budapest seemed safe enough. It was necessary for them to split up. There was no chance of their going to a hotel together, or even of finding a room somewhere that they might share. That sort of thing, Durell had decided, was far too dangerous. It was Ilona who had suggested that they each select an objective. She had a friend, she said, a man who had worked on the newspaper, *Szabad Nep*, who lived not far from the newspaper's office building in Pest, near Rakoczi Street and Jozsef Boulevard. She would contact him, using her old AVO papers, and try to learn in which prison McFee was being held. McFee was to be her target, because of her AVO connections. Dr. Tagy's whereabouts, if indeed the man were still alive, was Durell's objective.

"We're not far from where Endre Stryzyk's sister lives," Ilona said. "I'll take you there. She worked as a telephone operator on the night shift, and she may be at home at this hour. She may be able to help you. There's no use looking in the telephone directory for any of Tagy's family; they wouldn't be listed these days. But I'll check the police register, if I can get into the files, and see what I can find out. Maria Stryzyk, I think, knew the Tagy family. I don't know where her sympathies may be, and you will have to be careful with her. She speaks English, but she may still believe in the Communist regime. So don't take any chances with her."

"Where will we meet?" Durell asked.

"At Maria Stryzyk's apartment," she said.

"When?"

It was eight o'clock in the morning. "At noon?"

"All right. But I don't like your heading back into any AVO office."

She smiled. "I'm in less danger, after all, than you are. If you try to say one complicated sentence, you'll be spotted as a Westerner. At least, I can get around without attracting attention to myself, as long as I stay away from Deak Ferenc Square. That's the headquarters of the AVO where I used to report to, and where I was summoned to work with Bela Korvuth."

"Be careful," Durell said.

She gave him the address of the Stryzyk apartment on Gellert Hill, in the residential section of old Buda. "You can take the trolley from here. Don't talk to anyone. If someone tries to stop you, do anything to get away. Don't let them take you and find your wounded shoulder. They'll either assume you fought in the revolution, as an American, and that would break things wide apart; or they'll—"

"I know what they might do," Durell said. "I'm worried about you."

"At noon," she said. "Here comes your trolley."

She kissed his cheek lightly, smiled, and walked away.

The trolley Durell took was not very crowded. There was only one woman aboard, three men sitting apart from each other, and a uniformed police agent with the blue metal tabs of the AVO sitting in the farthest seat back. Durell seated himself halfway down the rocking car and watched the ruined streets speed by the window. He knew that what she was about to do was more dangerous than his immediate job, and he felt a deep admiration for her, and sympathy for the hours ahead of her. It was not easy for her to come back here where every hand was lifted against her, where her friends hated her as a member of the dreaded secret police, and where the police themselves would regard her as a traitor if she were discovered. He remembered her calm courage during their walk just now, and how she had been in the attic room during the night—a simple, frank and wonderful girl, hungry for love and security. An easy comradeship had been established between them, and he was no longer in doubt about whether he could trust her now. . . .

Buda, on the western bank of the Danube, was high and hilly, the residential, cultural side of the city as opposed to Pest, which had grown from a mud village in Roman times to a vast industrial and commercial complex. Now and then, from the narrow, hilly streets, Durell glimpsed the Danube itself, and the famous bridges—and everywhere were bombed and shelled houses, the rubble of destruction in the fierce, fantastic street fighting where youngsters tackled monstrous tanks with lengths of pipe, gasoline bottles, grenades, bricks, anything. Many of the fine trees lining the boulevards had been blasted to shattered stumps. And here and there, in the narrow cul-de-sacs among houses a thousand years old, were still the rusting ruins of tanks lured into traps between the ornate old buildings.

Durell got off at the street Ilona had indicated, and as he stepped off the trolley he was suddenly aware of movement behind him. In the reflection of the glass of the folding exit door he saw the uniform of the AVO man who had been sitting in the rear of the car. He did not turn around. Crossing to the sidewalk, he turned right immediately, in the opposite direction he wanted to go, his stride direct and certain, as if he knew his destination by rote. He found himself on a narrow, quiet residential street that had by some chance missed the worst of the fighting. Only a few chipped scars in the stone façades of the apartment houses indicated a few sniper's bullets had found their way here. The trees were bare, a delicate tracery of clean limbs overhead, making a shadow pattern on the old sidewalks.

Measured, booted footsteps followed him.

The street was empty in the bright, cold sunlight, except for a woman bundled in an old cloth coat, hurrying along the opposite sidewalk. It slanted sharply upward toward the ruins on Castle Hill, and Durell turned the next corner, a full block now from where the trolley had dropped him. The footsteps still trod in measured pace behind him. He saw that the street he had entered was a dead end, cut across the opposite end by a massive rococo apartment house. The windows had been shot out and the place looked empty and desolate. He went unhesitatingly to the front door.

"You, there!"

The AVO man's voice cut harshly across the sunny stillness. Durell turned on the steps. The man looked big, bulky and ominous in his warm uniform. His eyes were small under heavy, bushy black brows, and there was an arrogance in his deliberate tread as he closed the distance between them. "You. Come down here."

Durell came down the steps from the empty apartment house.

"What are you doing here?" the AVO man asked.

"Nothing."

"You live here?"

He gave the address of a building that was not that of Maria Stryzyk. "I live at No. Twenty-eight Tisza Square."

His accent was noticed. The man's eyes narrowed. "You are not from Budapest?"

"No. I come from Pecs. I am ill, that is why I am not working."

Pecs was where the Hungarian uranium mines were located.

The AVO man didn't like it. His mouth widened in a false smile. "Well, then, perhaps it is all right. Have you a match, comrade?"

"Of course."

Durell took out a small, engine-turned lighter. It was a cheap lighter of Swiss manufacture. The guard turned it over in thick, blunt fingers. "Where did you get this?"

"From a Russian soldier. He had many of them. We were drinking together one night, and he gave it to me as a gift."

"You speak strangely. You are a foreigner, aren't you?"

"Yes. I was brought in to work in the mines. I worked there for three years, until I got sick."

"Your papers," the AVO said bluntly.

Durell took out the papers he had been furnished in Spain. He looked beyond the man's bulky, uniformed figure and saw no one on the sunlit, cobblestoned street. There was faint movement at one of the windows nearby, but it vanished almost immediately. He looked at the agent's thick, brutal neck. There, he thought, is where I'll hit him. Just above that pulsing artery.

The guard returned his papers. "Everything seems in order. You are directed to stay out of empty buildings, do you understand? There is to be no more looting."

"Yes. I am sorry. I just thought I'd look around."

"Go home and stay there," the man said.

He pocketed Durell's lighter, as if in absent-minded gesture. Durell did not ask for its return. The big man turned and strode away, his new boots ringing on the cold cobblestones. Durell let out his breath slowly and walked after him to the corner, and when the other man turned left, Durell turned the other way.

The apartment house at No. 14 Tisza Square was five stories high, with ornate balconies of fat, rounded balustrades, carved gray stone lintels, and a grilled doorway. Tisza Square was little more than a wide area in the narrow street sloping up toward the crest of Castle Hill. Far away and down, he could see the Danube, and the smoke of factories on Csepel Island, the heavy-industry district, and the bridges where so much fighting had taken place. A cold wind blew from over the plains to the east. He searched the directory under the polished brass mailboxes, none of which contained any mail that he could see, found Maria Stryzyk's name, and thumbed the bell. The apartment number was 4-A and he did not wait for any response, but turned at once to the dark stairway and climbed to the fourth floor. The building was very quiet, and he met no one on his way up.

The door to Number 4-A was closed. He knocked, listened, heard nothing, and knocked again, a little more imperiously. Nobody appeared in the shadowed hallway, where elegance of wallpaper had deteriorated into faded patterns, peeling paint, and scarred plaster. The air felt cold and damp. He knocked again, more loudly, and called softly: "Maria, open up!"

This time he heard a hesitant footstep, then someone approached the door quickly and he heard bolts being withdrawn and then the door opened about two inches. He glimpsed a woman's face, pale with sudden fear as she saw his big figure, and he put a hand against the door panel and shoved hard, driving her back with a little gasp of terror as he forced his way in. He closed the door quickly behind him, threw the bolt again, and said: "Don't be afraid. I am not the police. I'm a friend."

The woman backed away from him. "I have no friends."

"Nevertheless, I am a friend. I mean you no harm." Durell saw her quick, terrified breathing and said suddenly in English: "I bring you news of your brother Endre."

He knew that what he had said was cruel; but it was necessary. Maria Stryzyk was a slender, dark-haired woman in her middle thirties. She might have been pretty once, and some of the fine contours of her facial structure still remained. Her eyes were wide and dark, bright with sudden hope, her mouth still shaken by quick fear. Her dark hair was pulled back severely from her oval face, and she clutched a faded gray flannel robe around her thin figure, as if she had been asleep or about to turn in. Then he saw suspicion replace the sudden hope in her dark eyes, and she spoke flatly, in Hungarian: "You are trying to trick me. My brother Endre was killed some time ago, here in Budapest, and he was buried with all the rest of them in a common grave."

"That's not quite true, Maria," Durell said gently. "Don't be afraid of me. I've come to you because I'm a stranger in Budapest and need help, and you are the only one I can turn to."

"Get out," she said. "Get out or I shall call for the police."

Durell said in English: "Endre was killed a few days ago, in the United States."

She stared at him with wide, uncomprehending eyes. She

raised both hands to her mouth, her fingers touching her quivering lips. Then she sat down suddenly, her thin body swaying from side to side, no longer looking at Durell, not looking at anything but a dead past. He moved away from the door and looked out through the window. The square below was quiet and peaceful in the winter sunlight. He saw nothing suspicious.

The apartment was simply furnished, with relics of a past comfort that had steadily deteriorated, like the apartment building itself. The radiators under the windows were almost stone cold. There was a door to the right and he looked through it into a small kitchen. Another door led into a tiny darkened bedroom. He went in there and looked into the ancient bath, saw cotton stockings hanging to dry, opened a closet door and saw three dresses, two cotton and one of red wool, and a woman's coat with a shabby fur collar, and one pair of flat-heeled woman's shoes. When he came back to the main room of the apartment, Maria Stryzyk had not moved.

"Maria," he said gently. "Make some coffee, if you have any."

"Yes, I have some."

"Go ahead, make a cup for yourself and for me."

She looked up at him, her eyes searching his face. "It is true? Endre is dead? He reached the United States, and he is dead now?"

"Yes. He was killed by an AVO agent there. In New Jersey."

Her mouth moved, then closed tightly. "And you? Who are you?"

"An American."

"A spy?"

"I do whatever is necessary. I've come to save someone. To bring him back to safety with anyone else who would like to join us."

"How can I trust you?" she whispered.

"You can't. I need help, and you can only listen to me and decide for yourself if you want to help."

She whispered: "Endre was only a boy. He was a child yesterday, and suddenly, overnight, when all the trouble started, he was a man, fighting and killing, shouting for freedom. He never knew what freedom was, yet it grew in his heart, planted there from something that lives in all men. I did not know he had escaped from Hungary. The police questioned me over and over again. They took me to the prison in Fo Street and kept me there for two months. I was very lucky. Things were confused. They were frightened, those beasts in the cellar prisons, and not sure of themselves. They broke my arm." She lifted her left arm and Durell saw that it had been broken and poorly set again. "But I was lucky. I came out of it alive. And poor Endre, just a boy, reached freedom and they followed him and killed him."

"Freedom is worth dying for," Durell said quietly. "Go on, get the coffee."

She stood up wearily. "Yes. I am sorry. You have come a long way, haven't you?"

"A very long way."

"If I can help you, I will."

"It will be dangerous for you," Durell said. "I can ask it only as a favor."

"If Endre died for what you work for, surely I can spare a little risk to myself. Life is hardly worth living these days, in any case." She was crying silently, her thin face tormented. "He was only a boy, do you understand? They were all children—fighting monsters, fighting for something they never had, and dying for it. For what I say to you, the AVO can kill me. They have killed many already who dreamed of a better life. If you came here to trick me, you can take me now. I am not sorry for anything I say or feel. I am only sorry we lost, that we had no help from you in the West, that we fought and died for nothing."

"It was not for nothing," Durell said. "It was a beginning."

"And an end for Endre."

She went into the small kitchen. Durell turned to the window and looked out at the small square below. A truck rumbled past, grinding up the steep hill in low gear. There were soldiers in it, men armed with automatic rifles, a machine gun mounted on the cab of the truck. The bright winter sunlight seemed to mock the impalpable darkness that shrouded this city. How many were like Maria? he wondered. How many were crushed and hopeless, how many still waited to fight again at some future time?

He went into the kitchen after Maria. She had put a gray enamel coffee pot on to boil and was staring at her hands in wonderment.

"Why was Endre killed?" she whispered. "Why was he hunted down so far away?"

Durell told her the circumstances of that morning in New Jersey. Not all of it, but enough so that it made sense and she understood what had happened. He knew that he was putting his life in her hands, but he had taken so many risks to reach this place that another was of small consequence. Maria listened without interrupting, her small face sober and pale, her dark eyes fixed on his face as if trying to weigh and assess the truth of what he was telling her. She believed him. She understood. When he was finished, the coffee was ready and she poured it into two cups and they went back to the living room.

"They had no right to kill Endre. He had fled, and he was out of it. It was just for revenge, for brutal killing, that he was murdered."

"Yes," Durell said.

"I still do not know why you are here, taking such awful chances to come to this city. If you are captured and discovered to be an American—"

"Do you know a family named Tagy?" Durell interrupted. "The family of a Dr. Tagy, who went to America some years ago?"

She nodded. "Yes, we are acquainted."

"Do you know where they are living now?"

"It is not far from here. Near Szena ter—it is in this section, too. But I have seen none of the family for several weeks."

"Would they trust you?"

She looked thoughtful. "I think so. You must understand how it is with us in this city. You suspect even your closest friends of being paid informers of the secret police. You never know who can be trusted, and so you say nothing, you speak banalities or you simply repeat phrases from the official propaganda line. And all the time as you look at the faces of your friends, you wonder what they are thinking, if they feel as you do about our terrible life, about the broken promises of the Communists, of the terror of the police and the rumors about the prisons. Yet you cannot speak. You don't dare.

"You may try, in a roundabout way, to sound out the true feelings of those you know, but even if they respond in a way that is hopeful to you, in hints and small indications that they feel as you do, you draw back suddenly, in quick fright, because it might be a trap." The dark-haired woman looked broodingly at her coffee. Her hands were restless. "But I have reached a point where I no longer care. When you came in an hour ago, I was like all the rest. And then you spoke in English and now I know that Endre is truly dead, and I have nothing more to lose. I will take you to the Tagy family."

Chapter Fourteen

I T WAS a half-hour walk through the hilly residential sections of Buda to the house Maria indicated. It was mid-morning now, after ten o'clock, and the city was a little more alive than it had been earlier. Maria walked briskly, her hands in the pockets of her thin, shabby coat, and she talked in aimless fashion about her job as a telephone operator on the night shift, of the days before the futile rebellion, of Endre as he had been as a schoolboy. Durell asked if she knew Ilona Andrassy and Maria's tone changed.

"I think Endre was in love with her once, but it was only a schoolboy affair, and when she went to work on the newspaper there were stories about her that I didn't like. It was said that she was an informer for the AVO. I have not seen her lately and I do not care to."

"She is working with me," Durell said. "She is here in Budapest. I think she can be trusted. Does that change anything?"

"I think you are a fool," Maria said. "The AVO are all beasts, perverts, sadists. The women who are in the AVO are even worse than the men."

"Yet she sent me to you, for help," Durell pointed out.

Maria's pale mouth grew thin. "Then perhaps this is the last day for us to see the sunlight."

"I don't think so. She's going to help us."

"Are you to meet her again today?"

"At your apartment. At noon."

Maria drew a deep, tremulous breath. Her thin, dark face was very intense. She could be dangerous now, Durell thought, filled with hatred because of the death of her brother. He hoped she knew how to control herself.

"I keep forgetting," Maria said. "I have already taken the final step, by accepting you and helping you. There can be no greater danger. If you believe in Ilona Andrassy, then I will take the chance, too. I want only one thing. I do not want to die before I do something, before I can strike one more blow for Endre."

"Perhaps the chance will come," Durell told her.

The place she took him to was not an apartment house, but a tall old house squeezed between houses of similar vintage on a narrow side street lined with barren, spidery poplar trees that bent in the cold wind that blew from the east. There was a medieval quality to the ancient street, and Durell knew from the narrow thoroughfares and haphazard layout of the surrounding streets that he was in one of the oldest parts of Buda that dated back to when the plains of Hungary represented the farthest outpost of the old Roman Empire civilization. He could see where the narrow streets and twisting alleys could represent perfect traps for destroying modern tanks.

"How come the Tagys rate a house?" he asked quietly.

"It has been in the family for many years. For generations."

"And it wasn't taken from them when Dr. Tagy fled to the West?"

"For a time, yes. But no one else lived in it, and when Eva Tagy was released from prison, along with her children, she was permitted to return here. She has been living here ever since."

"What about the children?"

"The little girl is gone. She disappeared. Probably she was killed last October. But there is a young son, Janos. About fifteen, I think. He was not involved in any of the fighting, because he was ill in the hospital with pneumonia at the time. It is the only thing that saved him from deportation, I'm sure."

They walked past the house. There were ornate balconies in front of the bay windows of the stone façade, and a steeply pitched tiled roof with ornate eave copings. Nothing stirred behind the windows. Like all the other houses in the city, it gave Durell the impression of sullen people hiding in silence behind locked doors.

"Do you think anyone is at home?"

"Mrs. Tagy will be there. The boy might be at school today. There is no place for the mother to go. She is rejected by the state, and refused anything but the most menial, hardest jobs. Someone is in there. We can go in the back way, if you wish."

They turned the corner into a narrow alley, a slot between high board fences in sad need of repair. Once there had been small, elegant gardens and terraces flourishing here, with views of the city below from this slope of hill; but ugly modern apartment buildings blocked out the view of the river now, and an air of desolation, neglect and decay was everywhere. They waited until a lone passenger car went by, one of the few Durell had seen in the city this morning, and then turned into the alley. Various gates opened into the wide back yards of the houses flanking the Tagy residence.

Maria paused at a small entranceway painted a faded green, and pulled on a small cord that vanished through a hole in the wooden fence. Somewhere a bell tinkled faintly. Nobody came to the gate. She pulled on the bell cord a second time, and then a door opened somewhere and then the gate was pulled open, too.

"Maria Stryzyk . . ." A small gray-haired woman huddled in an old pull-over sweater stood facing them. Her face was round and sweet, her eyes a dark gray in which quick fear flamed as her glance touched Durell's tall figure behind the woman.

"May we come in?" Maria asked quickly.

"Why do you come this way? What do you want?"

"We do not wish to attract attention. This man wants to talk to you."

The woman's mouth trembled and her hand crept to her throat. "The police? But—"

"Not the police," Durell said. "Please. We can't wait here."

Durell pushed open the gate and Maria slid quickly inside the little garden area. The woman stood to one side, an air of helplessness in the way she carried herself. Her face was very white.

"We have done nothing. Nothing at all," she said quickly. "You have no need to trouble us, we are good citizens—"

"It's all right, Eva," Maria said gently. "There is nothing to fear. But it is better if we go inside."

They crossed a small brick path between the bare tangle of shrubbery into a back door. The white-haired woman closed and locked the door behind them, told them to follow her, and they crossed a large, clean kitchen and went down a hallway to the front of the house.

"It is a long time since you have visited us, Maria."

"This man wants to talk to you. Is Janos at home?"

"He is upstairs in bed. He has a very bad cold."

"And no one else is here?" Maria asked.

"Who else is there?"

Durell said: "I am looking for your husband, Mrs. Tagy."

The woman halted in the middle of the front room of the house. A strange little animal sound came from her, but she did not turn to face Durell. Her whole posture was one as if he had suddenly struck at her with a knife. He could not see her face, since she stood with her back to him, but he saw the way her shoulders stiffened and he wondered how she had managed to dissemble and hide her secret as long as now, her nerves being what they were. He disliked frightening her, and he was not even sure that he was using the right approach, since if she distrusted him she could prove stubborn and waste time that was too precious to lose. He walked up to her and took her shoulders gently in his hands.

"It's all right. I am not of the police. Believe me. I wish no harm to you or your husband. I've come here to help him. I've come a long way to find him and talk and help him do what he came here to do. Do you understand me?"

"No. Dr. Tagy is not here. He has been gone three years. You know that. Why do you ask about him now?"

"Because he is here. We know he is in Budapest. Perhaps he is hiding in this house. He will be safe with me. You will all be safe. I'll help him get you out of the country. That's what he came back for, isn't that so?"

He was not quite ready for her reaction. He did not know where she had hidden the knife. But she slipped away suddenly from his hands on her shoulders, and from somewhere inside her bulky sweater, the sweet-faced little woman took the knife and slashed violently at Durell. The blade flickered wickedly in the sunlight coming through the front bay windows. She was transformed, her face convulsed with despair and fear and rage, and a shrill screaming sound came from her open mouth. Durell parried the blow easily. He heard Maria shout something and from the tail of his eye he saw her jump forward, but he twisted the elderly woman's wrist easily, not wanting to hurt her, and although she struggled on for another moment, still screaming in Hungarian some words he could not understand, he forced the knife from her grip and when it fell to the bare wooden floor, he kicked it aside.

"Please, Mrs. Tagy," he said. "Believe me. I wish you no harm."

Her breathing was wild and tumultuous. She stood before him with her eyes closed, her throat moving as she swallowed. "You can kill me, but I will never tell you anything."

"I will not kill you. I won't hurt you."

"You are the police. This woman brought you here. How much did you pay her for the information? Or did you threaten her with your horrible prisons to make her bring you to me?"

"Neither one. Listen to me. Sit down. Didn't you understand what I said. I know Dr. Tagy came back to Budapest to help you. He was working for us—for America, the same as I do. Now do you understand? I came back here because he did not return with you. I don't know why he failed, I don't even know if he was lucky enough to reach you. But I must find him, before the AVO gets on his trail. They sent a man to the United States to kidnap or kill him, whichever suited them best. They didn't know he had come back here. But they will know soon. They will come here for you, for him and for your son—"

"Get away from my mother!"

It was a boy's voice, directed at Durell's back, but there was something in the tone and the words that made him stand quite still. The white-haired woman sank down on a chair and covered her face. Her breath made a tortured sound in the sudden stillness.

"Janos?" Durell said.

"Turn around. Easily. Or you are a dead man."

The boy stood in the doorway, near the foot of the stairs that led to the upper floor of the house. He was thin and spindly, not more than fifteen, all arms and legs and bony wrists. The snubby-barreled "Russian guitar" in his hands was held competently, and there was on his narrow face a blazing look of furious hatred that left Durell no doubt that he stood dangerously close to death.

Maria whispered, "Janos, don't!"

"Get away, Maria. I'm going to finish him," the boy whispered.

"Did you hear what I told your mother?" Durell asked.

"I heard. You are a liar, like all the rest of them."

"Put down that gun," Durell said. "I'm a friend."

"That's what the Russians said, before they turned their tanks on us and crushed us under the treads. Do you know something? I, myself, blew up two of their tanks. When they came up Castle Hill, we lured them into a dead-end street and we filled the hollows of the street with gasoline and when the tanks splashed through we gave them a grenade or two. That finished them. That's how I got this gun. I took it off a Russian I killed. A man like you."

Durell wanted the boy to keep talking, but the mother murmured something and he broke off abruptly, his pale eyes suddenly uncertain. Maria said something in Hungarian that Durell did not understand. He felt a cool sweat on his face and he knew he was afraid of this boy who had killed Russian tanks. There was a wildness in Janos Tagy that was beyond any reason. Only his mother's voice kept his finger quiet on the trigger.

"I believe him, Janos," Mrs. Tagy whispered. "Even if he lies, it must come to this end. If he tells the truth, then we must decide now, once and for all, what to do about your father."

"Is he here?" Durell asked.

The woman looked at him with round, dead eyes. "Yes."

"Alive?"

"He almost died. He was sick and wounded. He was wounded by a border guard when he came through. And then he became feverish and the wound was infected and we hid him here. It was only by the grace of God that he found strength to make his way to this house. He came in the night, and nobody saw him, and we have been hiding him here ever since."

"Take me to him," Durell said. "Janos?"

The boy still hesitated, but the muzzle of his gun was lowered now. His mouth shook uncertainly as he looked from his mother to Durell. Then he shrugged his thin shoulders. His eyes were still wild.

"I will take him, if you say so, mother. But I will kill him if he touches you again."

"It was not his fault," the woman said wearily. "Come, we will all go. He must have heard my screaming. He will be worried."

Durell moved ahead at a gesture from the boy's gun. To his surprise, they did not go upstairs, where the boy had come from. They returned to the kitchen, where the woman opened a cellar door and Durell was forced to lead the way down. The cellar felt warmer than the upper floors of the house. The walls were of massive stone, the floor of earth, and a huge coal furnace stood silent and black in one corner. Durell felt Maria touch his arm in what was meant to be reassurance, but he saw that her face was drawn tight, the skin shiny over her prominent cheekbones, her mouth set in an uncompromising line. The thought flashed through his mind that she may well have led him here to his death. Yet he did not seriously doubt her. He felt the boy, Janos, prod him again with the muzzle of the Russian gun.

"Go ahead. Into the furnace."

"The furnace?"

"There is a trap door inside. A long time ago, a hundred years ago, we Hungarians rebelled against tyranny, too." The boy's voice was thin and proud. "Those were the days of Petoefi, and General Bems. There were heroes in the land then, and there will be more heroes again." He paused. "In those days there was fighting here, too. They built tunnels to get from one house to another, and most of them are forgotten today. But I found this one, years ago, and we fixed it up with the furnace to hide the entrance."

"Then you have no heat in the house?" Durell asked.

"We can build a fire quickly on the steel plate inside, if we have to. It is the same plate that acts as the trap door. Go ahead, climb inside. And be careful, I will be directly behind you. I don't care if I have to die, too."

Durell believed him. There was a brave, wild immaturity in Janos Tagy, but there was also a grim sense of responsibility beyond his years. Durell opened the wide furnace door. There was easily enough room for him to climb inside, and he saw the steel plate clearly on the floor of the furnace, with a ring-bolt set in it that lifted easily when he pulled it up. A dark opening and the top rungs of a wooden ladder were revealed. He squeezed inside and climbed down.

Light flickered downward over him, and he looked back and saw that Janos had taken a flashlight to guide the way. There were more than a dozen rungs to the ladder, and then he had to drop three feet to a brick floor. The tunnel stretched in both directions, brick-walled, with a vaulted ceiling. Water dripped somewhere, but it was not as cold as the outer air.

"To your right," the boy whispered. "And do not make a sound for fifty paces. We will be going under the neighbors' cellars, and they do not know about this passage. But they might hear. So be careful."

Durell led the way. He heard Maria climb down after him, and then Mrs. Tagy, and he wondered suddenly what would happen to them all if Roger Wyman's tip to the AVO should lead the secret police to this place now. The thought gave him a renewed sense of urgency, of time slipping by that could never be regained. He went ahead, a sense of excitement and anxiety mixed in him that he always felt when he was near a goal in his mission. The light flickered erratically, then focused on a wide area of the tunnel ahead. He saw a cot, a heap of blankets, a small table and an oil lamp, and quickened his stride to look down at the man who lay with his face to the damp, brick tunnel walls.

It was Dr. Tagy.

Chapter Fifteen

"HOW LONG has he been like this?" Durell asked. He spoke to Janos Tagy. "He looks as if he's under drugs."

"Yes. To make him sleep. He should wake up soon."

"Can he walk?"

"Yes, a little. But he is not strong enough yet to try to cross the frontier with us."

"You planned to leave with him?"

"He came back for us," the boy said proudly. "He could not take Mama and me the first time. But when all the fighting began, he came back to rescue us." The thin shoulders slumped in despair. "But he was wounded and sick. We had to hide him down here. Every now and then the police come and look through the house. So far, they have not taken Mama or me to the cellar prisons. They search, and find nothing, and go away."

"When was the last time they were here?"

"Two days ago."

"Do you expect them soon?"

The boy shrugged again. "One never knows with those animals. They show up at any time, at any hour."

"And you kept your father down here all this time?"

"Yes. All this time. Mama and I nursed him. He's much better, actually. We thought perhaps we could try for the frontier in another week or so."

"You had no friends who could help you before this?"

"There is no one to trust," Janos said simply.

"And now your time has run out," Durell said. "Until now, the AVO had no real reason to believe your father was back in Budapest. But they know now. In an hour, perhaps sooner, they will come back and this time they will get the truth from you, Janos."

"Not from me," the boy said tightly. His smile was grim. "They may kill me, but they will not make me talk."

"And your mother?" Durell asked. His voice was quiet. "Would you be silent if you were forced to watch them torture your mother?"

Janos's gaze faltered. He bit his lip. The gun he carried sagged, and he looked uncertainly at the small, white-haired woman, at Maria, and then at the sleeping man on the cot. His mouth shook.

"I don't know," he whispered. "Perhaps not—I couldn't stand—"

"Then you have to trust me," Durell said flatly. "There isn't time for you to think about it. All of you will have to come with me."

"Now?" Mrs. Tagy asked faintly.

"At once. Maria, will you take the risk of hiding these people in your apartment until tonight?"

The dark-haired girl nodded. "If we can get them there."

"Janos, is there another way out of this tunnel?" Durell asked.

"Yes, but I left so many things in the house—"

"Leave them there and forget them. It will be better if it looks to the police as if you just walked out and expect to return any moment. Come on, help me get your father awake."

There were several precious minutes lost while the wife and son shook and talked to the sick man. Dr. Tagy had a round face like his wife's, but there were deep lines etched at the mouth and an unhealthy color to his cheeks. He was unshaven, and his beard glinted silvery-gray in the light of the lantern. Durell walked carefully back down the tunnel to the trap in the coal furnace by which they had entered. Listening for a moment, he heard no sound, and then climbed the ladder and returned to the cellar above. He checked the back door, went out into the glare of sunlight in the garden to lock the gate; then he returned, closing the cellar door, climbed back through the huge furnace door and carefully drew the steel plate shut over his head.

He wondered how much time he really had. He did not know, actually, if McFee had let anything slip to Roger Wyman in Vienna, but a report from Wyman to AVO headquarters here, yielding his own identity, would set the wheels in motion, connecting him to Bela Korvuth's mission, and in turn, bringing Dr. Tagy's name into it. He did not underestimate the enemy. The top echelons of the secret police were fanatic, intelligent, dedicated men. On the surface, his hope for success was too small even to consider. Yet he had to try. He had come this far, somehow, with luck and Ilona's help, and he had found willing hands to carry on, in Maria and the Tagy family. Yet when he thought of Roger Wyman and of Dickinson McFee in some prison, being questioned and tortured, he felt the nerves tense in the back of his neck and he paused until the wave of anger passed and he felt calm again.

Dr. Tagy was on his feet when he returned. The man was short; even Maria stood taller than he. He looked haggard and confused, but his eyes sharpened as Durell approached down the tunnel.

"You are the American?"

"Yes. How do you feel?"

"Well enough to go, with a man's help. I have been a fool. All this time lost because I was unlucky enough to catch a bullet in my leg at the frontier, and then fell sick, like a weakling."

"You could have told our security people how you felt about your family," Durell said. "Some arrangements could have been made to help get them out to you."

Dr. Tagy groped for his glasses on the bunk and put them on. His wife supported his weight as he limped and stumbled. "I am a man of science, and perhaps not very practical when it comes to simple human relations. I simply wanted to make sure for myself that my wife and son were safe. Instead, I bungled everything. I risked my own life and put them in gravest danger. Now, of course, you have come to help and everything will be all right."

Durell did not want to tell him he was being overoptimistic. They were a long way from being safe. And when he saw that Dr. Tagy could make only slow and painful progress on his feet, his concern was doubled. His son supported him now, indicating that they should proceed down the tunnel away from the direction they had come.

Dr. Tagy spoke again, pausing for breath after they had gone only a short distance. "I am grateful to you, sir, but I begin to think that what you are trying to do is impossible. Perhaps I had better stay here for a few weeks more, until my strength has returned."

"No, Papa," Janos said. "You come with us."

"I can bring only disaster to you, this way." Dr. Tagy

halted, swaying. "Perhaps you, sir, will take my wife and son to the frontier." He looked at Durell in resignation. "At least, then, I will know they are safe."

"I am afraid we consider you more important than anyone else."

"But you see how I am. It is a long way, and dangerous, to the frontier. I will only cause you all to be caught. Leave me here, sir, I beg you. Take my wife and Janos."

"We all get out, or none of us," Durell said. "There is no time to argue. Janos, where does this tunnel take us?"

"We can climb out in an empty house the Russians shelled. There were snipers there, and the tanks fired point-blank at the building. No one will see us."

"Do you think you can possibly find a car?"

The boy nodded. "We hid one during the fighting. I think it belonged to some AVO men. It is behind a wall in the rubble, near the tunnel exit."

"Go ahead then, and get it. Bring it around so we get your father into it."

The boy shifted the gun in his hand and looked uncertain. His father nodded. "Go, Janos."

"I don't like to leave you, Papa."

"I will be all right with the American."

The exit from the tunnel required less contortions than the entrance in the Tagy cellar. There was a sharp tunnel in the brick-lined walls and then a glimpse of pale white sunlight. Janos pushed aside some heavy planking and then stepped free, onto a vast pile of shattered brick, stone and timbers. Durell saw that they stood inside the shell of a shattered building, one wall of which had completely collapsed, the others being only skeletal fragments standing precariously in the bright sunshine. Nobody else was in sight. He helped Dr. Tagy climb free, and then Eva Tagy and Maria. Janos silently handed his Russian gun to Durell, and then went scrambling out of sight among the rubble. Durell looked at his watch. It was almost eleven o'clock. The sun stood high in the morning sky. A small sparrow landed with a flutter of gray wings and perched on a splintered timber and cocked its small head at him, eyes bright and inquiring. Durell sat down, aware of a new, pulsing ache in his wounded-shoulder; he wished for a cigarette, but he knew it was impossible, and he contented himself with drawing in deep breaths of the cold, fresh air. Maria started to say something and he beckoned her to silence. There was no telling who might be passing by on the other side of the ruined walls.

They waited five minutes. And then ten.

Durell moved to a gaunt window opening and risked a glimpse of the street beyond. It was narrow, slanted and twisting, like all the old streets in this hilly part of Buda. Two men stood talking and smoking at the far corner, near the splintered remains of a tree. He saw trolley tracks and wires at the intersection, but while he watched there were no trolleys that passed, and only one truck and one car. The car was moving fast, and it turned out of sight at the corner, going downhill, and he could not see who was in it except for the impression that it was crowded with men.

Durell looked back at the trio sitting on the rubble, waiting with him. The two women were whispering, Maria's dark face thin and intense. Dr. Tagy sat with his hands dangling limply between his knees. He looked broken and defeated. Durell turned his head as the sound of a car came grinding up the cobblestone street from the bottom of the hill. The two men talking on the corner were gone. There were no other signs of life in the street. When he saw the car, his hopes sagged for a moment. It was an old Zis sedan, Russian-made, battered and bullet-scarred. It would be too conspicuous on the streets. Yet there was no other choice. Dr. Tagy was too weak and feeble to hope to walk to Maria Stryzyk's apartment, and public transportation was out of the question. They would have to risk it.

Janos looked flushed and jubilant as he rejoined them. "I have been thinking about everything. We will take Papa and Mama to Maria's right now, and I will return the car to its hiding place. Then, tonight, we will use it to get to the frontier. We are armed, there are enough of us to help each other. It is best that we get out of the city quickly."

Durell had no intention of leaving until he found out from Ilona what had happened to Dickinson McFee; but he did not mention this. There were two or three long, tight minutes when they had to leave the shelter of the ruined house and cross the paving to the parked sedan. If anyone saw them, there was no immediate alarm. Janos ran around to the driver's side and slid happily behind the wheel. The boy seemed different, excited by the action after all the weeks of hiding and struggling to keep his father's presence a secret from prying neighbors. Yet he drove competently, not too fast to attract attention, and not too slow to waste time.

There was another hurdle to be passed in getting them all up to Maria's apartment. It was decided that they would go one or two at a time. Maria and Eva Tagy got out of the car first, around the corner, and walked into the building while Janos circled the block in the car and doubled back. Then Durell helped Dr. Tagy, supporting him as inconspicuously as possible until they crossed the sidewalk into the building. Janos drove the car away and promised to be back in twenty minutes, after hiding it again.

Inside the apartment, Dr. Tagy was made to rest in Maria's bedroom. Maria made more coffee and set out bread and cheese for their lunch. Mrs. Tagy sat beside her husband on the bed.

Durell checked the apartment doors again, studied the view from the window, and settled down to wait. At eleven-thirty Maria came toward him, smiling, and suggested he bathe and shave, and he was glad of the chance. By noon he was watching from the window again, waiting for Ilona.

Janos did not come back.

Neither did Ilona.

Durell drank coffee and ate a sandwich and went in to look at Dr. Tagy. The little physicist was asleep. He seemed slightly feverish. His wife regarded Durell with anxious eyes.

"Didn't Janos say he would be back at once?"

"He'll be all right. He's a fine boy, Mrs. Tagy. We can count on him to take care of himself."

"But it is the hate in him that makes me worry. His hatred makes him do reckless things. He does not stop and think or count the cost. He should have been back by now."

"He'll be back," Durell said gently.

At one o'clock there was no sign of either Ilona Andrassy or the boy.

It was nothing to jump the rails about, Durell thought. In this business there were times of waiting and times of action, and it was necessary to be able to do one as well as the other. You can't afford to think or dwell on what might be happening to those you were waiting for. Either they showed up or they didn't. You gave them a reasonable time, and then a little extra time, and then if it was necessary to change your plans, you did so.

He had waited like this many times before, and it was never easy. Sometimes your patience was rewarded. At other times, you had to accept the grim evidence before you and retreat, abandon the ones you hoped to see again, and go on. You always had to go on, one way or another, and not look back and wonder if this could have been done, or if that course might have worked better, or if this one would be alive today if you had acted, somehow, in a different manner. You planned and you carried out the plan, and if some of it didn't work, you tried something else.

Ilona would come back. She had to.

He remembered how she had been the night before, in the attic room of the Hegedus farm. There was something fine and wonderful in the simple relationship that had built up so quickly between them. He wanted very much for her to come through this safely, to find what she wanted, to hold this thing she sought that she had never known in all her life. She had not been forced to come back here with him, to this place of terror and death. She had known the risks, the special dangers for herself, and she had agreed to his question with a simple nod, swallowing her fear. There was a strength in her that he marveled at, thinking about the painful conclusions she had reached alone in her own soul. Freedom was something Ilona had never known. It had been within her grasp, back in Washington; she could have been safe there. But she had returned to Budapest with him, and she was his responsibility, no matter what denials she might make about it.

The street was empty. She did not come back. There was no sign of Janos, and it was two o'clock now, two hours late, and it was time to think of what he could do without her.

Dr. Tagy was asleep. His wife sat in quiet terror beside him. Maria joined Durell at the window, her thin figure severe and prim, her voice quiet.

"What if Ilona doesn't come back?" she asked quietly. "She is very late now. If it is known that she works for the West now, and is regarded as a traitor by her former associates in the AVO, it will go very very hard with her if she is caught."

"We'll have to do without her, if she doesn't meet us here."

"And the boy? What about Janos? We need the car."

Durell looked at her. "You talk as if you're willing to come with us."

"There is nothing left here for me in Budapest. I have no relatives, no friends. If you will take me, I will go to the West with you."

"Do you know of another car we might be able to use?"

She shook her dark, narrow head. "No. And I do not think you could persuade Dr. Tagy and his wife to flee without their son."

"We'll wait until dark before we decide," Durell said.

"I have been watching you. You need Ilona. There is something else you want to do here in Budapest, besides rescue Dr. Tagy. Isn't that so? Something, perhaps, more important than the doctor. Are you really a spy? Are there any secrets you wish to take with you?"

"No. No secrets, Maria."

"Don't misunderstand me. I hate the Russians. I hate what they have done to my poor country. Our men who are in the government are only pawns, paying lip service to the conception of their being independent, but all the time the Russians sit behind them and pull the strings and tell them what to say and do. If you can hurt them in any way, I will help you."

"That's not my job here," Durell said. "I have to find a friend. I'm sure he's in one of the AVO prisons here, and Ilona set out to learn which one."

Maria's mouth thinned. "She went back to the AVO?"

"I think so."

"Then they have her, and there is no use waiting for her. You can only pray that she will die quickly."

"We'll wait and see," Durell said.

He didn't like it. In the past, when he had to wait like this, he had been able to sit with measured patience, ignoring the time, the dragging hours, the uncertainty. Here, in this place, he felt trapped and futile. He had the feeling that things were moving beyond his reach and control, and every now and then he wondered about Dickinson McFee, in the hands of the AVO. He had known the little man for almost ten years, and while he would not have admitted it to anyone, he felt almost a love for McFee, for the little gray man's devotion, intelligence, dedication to the job he did. McFee had been good to him more than once, had helped him at times when cool and calculating reason should have ordered his abandonment. He could not leave here without McFee. If McFee were already dead, that was one thing. But if he were alive, if he was being tortured at this moment, Durell had to help him. He had to do something, and yet he could not move for these long, desperate hours of the afternoon, there was no place he could go or start until he definitely gave up hope for Ilona.

It was late afternoon before he saw Janos's battered old car. Nothing had changed in the apartment. Dr. Tagy had wakened, eaten some soup that Maria prepared for them all, and then he went back to sleep again. Nobody had disturbed them, and it was growing dark, with a thin overcast in the western sky over the city, when Durell saw the old Zis turn the corner.

His pulse jumped erratically for a moment, then settled down. He had not realized how anxious he had been about the boy. The car came grinding slowly up the hill and then halted directly in front of the apartment house, which Durell did not like.

Maria joined him at the window. "It's Janos?"

"I think so."

The boy got out from behind the wheel, his thin freckled face smiling. Something seemed to be different about him, but Durell could not spot what it was. Then someone else got out of the car, and it took a long moment before he recognized who it was. It didn't make sense.

"Who is the girl?" Maria whispered.

The girl who joined Janos on the sidewalk had dark, raven-black curls in a rather severe cut, worn under a small suede beret. She had on a lined trenchcoat, belted tightly about her waist, and dark blue shoes. She said something to the boy, and Janos nodded and waved toward the door of the building and she passed from sight.

"It's Ilona," Durell said. "She's taken time to dye her hair black."

"Are you sure?"

"Yes, I'm sure."

The sudden quickening of elation in him then came to a sudden halt. Someone else was in the car. It was a man, bulky of shoulder, massive in his blue uniform. The man paused on the sidewalk with his hand on Janos's slim shoulder and looked directly up at the bay window where Durell watched. Everything seemed to come to a halt inside Durell. He heard Maria gasp in sudden fear.

The man with Janos was an AVO guard. Durell recognized the broad jaws, the thick black line of bushy brows over clever, suspicious eyes.

It was the same AVO man who had halted him and questioned him near the Tagy house that morning.

Durell reached for the Russian tommy gun Janos had left with him.

Chapter Sixteen

DURELL closed the door to the bedroom where Dr. Tagy and his wife waited, then crossed the other room with a quick stride, the automatic rifle in his hand, and took up a position beside the front entrance. He waved Maria back and to one side. Maria Stryzyk looked pale and shaken. He motioned to her for silence as someone knocked on the door, quickly and lightly.

"Maria?" It was Ilona's voice. "Maria, let me in. Hurry."

Durell opened the door. There were heavy footsteps below, on the stairway going down to the street level, but Janos and the AVO man were not yet in sight. He caught Ilona's arm and pulled her swiftly inside. She looked quite different, and yet she was the same. Her smile was quick and tremulous, her brown eyes bright with relief as she came against him and kissed him.

"Thank God, you are safe. Did you find Dr. Tagy?"

"They're all here," Durell said. "Quickly now, who is the man with Janos?"

She saw his gun for the first time. "Put it away. He is a friend."

"No, he isn't. He stopped me this morning near the Tagy house."

"I know. He told me. His name is Matyas. He is a friend."

"How can you trust him?"

Ilona looked surprised. "How does one trust anybody here?"

"How did you meet Janos Tagy?"

"I went to the Tagy place, thinking you might still be there. Janos was alone in the house. He talked quite freely to me, after I let him know I was looking for you. He told me what you had done, and it is wonderful. Then the AVO man came in—Matyas—and I almost died of fright. Janos held a knife to his throat, surprising him from behind. But there was no need to be afraid. He pleaded with us to take him along. He said he had been following you all day, since early morning, when we got off the train at the station."

There was no time for further questions. Janos came bounding up the stairs, his face joyous, and he was followed

121

by the heavy, deliberate tread of the AVO guard. The man's
heavy face smiled tentatively, and he held out his hands,
palm forward, at Durell's gun.

"Please. Trust me. I beg of you, believe me, I am a friend."

"Get in here," Durell said shortly. "If you're not alone,
you're a dead man. Do you understand that?"

"Of course. I assure you, nobody will follow."

"Assure yourself of that, not me. Get over there and sit
down."

Janos had gone into the bedroom to join his parents. Maria
drew a deep, uncertain breath and took the gun from Durell
and stood covering the AVO man. Her face was momentarily
convulsed with hatred.

"I think we should kill him, just to be sure."

"Wait, please," Matyas whispered. "Ilona, tell them. Tell
them how I could have arrested you several times over."

"Maybe you just wanted her to lead you here," Durell
suggested.

"No, it is not so. Tell him, Ilona! This woman wants to
kill me!"

"It would be too good for you, killing with bullets," Maria
said thinly. Her face was tight and hard. "That uniform
makes me sick to my stomach."

"But it will be very useful to us, Maria." Ilona spoke
quietly, placatingly. She took off her small suede beret and
shook her newly black, shining curls free. Durell had difficulty
adjusting to the change in her appearance. He saw that she
had also picked up a large handbag somewhere, and now she
took several bottles from it and put them on a table. "These
are for you, darling," she told Durell. "It seems that our
description has been circulated throughout Budapest. It came
through from Austria about noon. You can guess from whom
the description came. Apparently, last night all that was available to the police was the simple flash warning that an enemy
agent and a woman might be found at Geza Hegedus's farm.
Our friend in Vienna could use a better communication
system, I suppose. Or perhaps he was too hurried and surprised by our appearance to make thorough arrangements last
night. However, he made up for it this morning. There isn't
a chance for us to go anywhere in this city without being
recognized and arrested. You will have to dye your hair,
darling. Since mine was red, I changed to black. You will
have to become a blond. I am sure Maria will help. It is
simple, as a disguise, but we can only hope it will work."

Durell nodded. "Did you contact your friend, Aczel, at Szabad Nep?"

"I had to wait until noon, when he came out of the building for lunch. I was afraid to go in before then, because there were too many people there who might have recognized me, and among them there could have been one who knew of my assignment with Bela Korvuth. That would have finished everything. But when Aczel came out, I talked to him and learned I could trust him. I had to wait another hour while he made inquiries. It had to be done carefully, but Aczel has friends in high places, among the puppet administration. He is in love with me, in case you wonder why he was willing to help."

"What did he learn?" Durell asked.

"Your little friend who was captured and trapped night before last at Györ was taken to the Fo Street prison here in Budapest. Then he was transferred to the main AVO headquarters at Sixty Stalin Ut. He is still there, being questioned."

"Is he still alive, Ilona?"

"Oh, yes. They will not kill him. They may not even use physical torture on him just now. They know who he is, you see. They know they have caught a tremendously important fish in their net. They may use psychological torture, and surely they have begun to use drugs on him, but Major Ulitsky, the Soviet MVD man who is really in charge of the AVO now, is quite elated by it all. He has given strict orders that McFee is not to be physically injured. Great plans are afoot for a tremendous propaganda trial that will show the world it was Western fascists and capitalistic warmongers who stirred up the trouble in October."

Durell faced the news grimly. Worse than anything, worse than the loss of Dr. Tagy, or Ilona, or the escape of Bela Korvuth, this could tear things wide apart. His eyes were dark and sober as he looked at Ilona.

"What chance is there of getting him out of Stalin Ut."

"None whatever, as long as he is there."

"You said something about Matyas's uniform being useful."

"Yes. They are going to move McFee this afternoon."

"Do you know where?"

"To a small prison on the outskirts of Pest. They are taking him across the Kossuth Bridge about four o'clock. There won't be a chance to touch him while he's being transferred."

"Why are they moving him?"

Ilona shrugged. "It was Major Ulitzky's orders. Apparently, the Russians don't trust the AVO to handle the matter properly. I understand the smaller prison, in Rezd, is run entirely by the MVD."

"Do we have a chance there?"

"Possibly. We will have to plan it very carefully," Ilona said. "It is a far greater chance that we will all be killed."

"It has to be done," Durell said. "We have to try."

"Yes, I know that."

"What time do you think would be best?"

"Perhaps at seven. Aczel said a very important Russian is flying here from Moscow tonight, to take personal charge of the interrogation. Once that happens, nothing more will be possible. Our chance will be lost. But the transfer to Rezd will be after the evening meal, about five o'clock. Say between six and seven. That will be best."

Durell looked at the big figure of the AVO guard. The man was sweating, uneasy in the face of Maria and the burp gun. The man looked tough and brutal, with his broad, scarred face, his heavy brows, his wide, hard mouth. But that didn't have to mean anything, he thought. There was a plea in the man's eyes, a tight and desperate demand for understanding.

"You say you followed this girl and me this morning?" he asked.

"Yes, comrade, when you first—"

"We are not comrades."

"I am sorry. It is a habit." Matyas swallowed noisily and held up his big hands. "Let me join you. Let me help you. I wanted to talk to you when I stopped you before, when you gave me your lighter in front of that ruin on Castle Hill. I knew what you were. I knew your story about being ill, and having worked in Pecs, was false. I could tell from your accent that you are a foreigner. And I also knew you were a very brave man to come here."

"You have things pretty much your own way in your job here," Durell said. "Why give it up to join us?"

"I want to. My brother—he is in New Haven. In America. He left long ago. I should have gone with him, but things were too easy for me, as you say. I have done many things I have been ashamed of, but believe me, I tried to help those who came my way. I don't want to be hated by my own people. It is a lonely thing, to walk the streets and see how people hate you. I never knew—I never dreamed how it was, until the fighting began. Ever since then I have been afraid."

Durell glanced at Maria. The dark-haired woman seemed uncertain. Her gun was lowered. Ilona decided it.

"We may need his uniform," she said. "And his papers, for tonight. It is true, we could kill him now and be as well off, but Matyas is also a strong man, and we will need strength. You have only yourself, and Janos, who is a boy. Dr. Tagy will need help. And the three of us—Maria, Mrs. Tagy and myself—we are only women. It is too much of a burden for you to carry alone, my dear. I think we can take a chance with Matyas."

Durell nodded and agreed.

His hair and mustache were blond by six o'clock, rinsed and soaped several times to dispel the sharp odor of the peroxide Ilona had purchased. The long hours of waiting had dragged slowly by somehow in the crowded little flat. Maria had emptied the kitchen of whatever food they could carry, and Janos had gone out again and scrounged an extra can of gasoline from somewhere. The car stood undisturbed on the dark street below the apartment windows. Durell wore Matyas's uniform. Matyas was bulkier than Durell, but the clothing fit well enough to pass, and the man's papers carried no photo of himself and only a smudged description that could have passed for anyone after Durell had spent some minutes with pen and ink in changing some of the scrawled items.

Durell, Matyas and Ilona left the apartment at six-fifteen. Maria remained behind with the Tagys, although Janos objected strenuously to being forced to stay. There was no place for him in Durell's plan. Matyas wore Durell's clothes, and Durell carried the "Russian guitar" and his own gun as well. Matyas was unarmed. Ilona had the AVO man's pistol.

Durell drove, following Ilona's directions. The way led down the hills of Buda and across the Kossuth Bridge over the Danube into Pest, then out along the boulevard named Rackoczi Ut. There was only light traffic. The city seemed darkened by the despair of terror still clinging to it. In the industrial outskirts of Pest, Ilona directed him into a side road that led to the factory suburb where the prison stood. The night was very dark, thanks to the overcast that had come up in the evening, but it was not as cold as it had been. Presently the houses and buildings thinned out, and fields and a few farms came into evidence. In another mile they came to the barbed wire surrounding the prison.

The place had been one of the minor estates of the Karolyi nobility, a gloomy and forbidding pile of masonry with castellated walls and watch turrets with slotted windows. Spotlights played in an irregular pattern inside the wire fencing beyond the main gates. Two T-54 tanks were parked off the road here, and a truckload of soldiers stood shivering in the raw wind, waiting to start for some unknown destination. Striped wooden bars were lowered across the road.

Boldness and speed, Durell knew, were their only chances for success. He got out of the car, slamming the door loudly, and strode toward the barrier. Over the pounding of his heart he heard the soldiers in the truck muttering, and one of them laughed, and then he stepped into the sentry's booth with his papers in his hand. The sentry was a stout, pig-eyed man in a fur uniform cap and a muffler around his throat.

"Colonel Sandor to see Major Ulitzky, at once."

The sentry said: "Major Ulitzky hasn't arrived yet."

"We know that. We will go in and wait."

The sentry saw nothing wrong with his uniform or his papers. He nodded and raised the barrier. Durell turned and walked back to the car and got in beside Matyas. Ilona was in the back seat, sitting stiffly and quietly. Durell drove through the gateway onto the prison grounds. There was a deep, muddy trench, like a moat, surrounding Rezd Prison, and the tires rumbled hollowly as they crossed it on a wooden bridge. Then another barbed wire barrier, and another sentry. Durell remained in the car and impatiently waved his papers at the guard from the car window. He was beckoned on, and drove up an asphalt road in a long curve that mounted a knoll and ended in front of the main entrance to the grim, medieval building.

Ilona and Matyas got out with him. Matyas had given Durell an intimate picture of the prison layout, and Durell moved forward with a sure step toward the guard room, to the right on the first floor. Several uniformed men lounging in chairs stood up at attention, and Durell ignored them, turning to a lieutenant behind a desk in one corner of the big barren chamber. The lieutenant was young, with a thin and ratty face, clever eyes, and a scar that ran down one cheek into his throat. His eyes flicked from Durell to Matyas and rested for a long moment on Ilona.

"Yes, Colonel?"

"We are here to confer with Major Ulitzky. I know he hasn't arrived yet, but there are some questions we must ask your special prisoner." Durell slapped a glove impatiently against his thigh. "You have a room available where we can interrogate him? I dislike the cellars."

"Many men are squeamish about the cellars, Colonel. You have a rather strange accent, sir. Are you Russian, may I ask?"

"Czech," Durell said. "Your prisoner conducted an operation in my former country that I have been requested to investigate."

The lieutenant looked confused. "Yet you wear our uniform?"

Durell's eyes were dark with anger as he swung toward the lieutenant's desk. "Do you question me?"

"No, no. It is just that—this is a very special man, sir. He only just arrived from the Fo Street central. Unfortunately, they were using hypnotic drugs on the man—I understand he is very stubborn, and our ordinary methods are forbidden. He is still under sedation."

"I wish to see him at once."

The lieutenant's mouth was thin and uncertain. "And this man and woman with you?"

"They are part of my staff. My secretary and aide."

"I see. Will you come this way, please?"

The lieutenant got up from his desk and led them down a long stone corridor. Dim, muffled sounds echoed through the building, like the ghosts of anguished and tormented souls. A man laughed somewhere, on a high-pitched, irrational note. Someone was screaming, but the sound was muffled by many thick stone walls. There was a strong odor of lye and other antiseptics, of sweat and urine and leather polish.

The lieutenant led them to a small room that contained two desks and two chairs and nothing more. The floor, the walls were of stone. The windows were barred. The naked light bulb and a lamp on one of the desks provided the only light.

"Wait here, please. All of you."

"My business is urgent," Durell reminded him.

"Of course, Colonel. It will only be a moment. Please wait."

He was gone, closing the door after him. The door was heavy, sheathed with steel plate over the old oak framework. It closed with a thick sound of finality. Durell found his hands sweating. His throat felt dry. He looked at Ilona and saw that her face was pale and uncertain. Matyas was scowling, his heavy black brows furrowed.

"I am not happy about this, Colonel," Matyas whispered.

"We must be patient," Durell said loudly. "There is always

a stupid routine to be followed. The lieutenant is a conscientious man."

Ilona whispered, "I don't like the way he looked at me."

"An old friend?"

"I don't know."

Two or three minutes went by. Durell wanted to go to the door and open it and look out, but mainly he wanted to know if it had been locked after the lieutenant left. He had the feeling that it was locked. He had not liked the sly look in the lieutenant's eyes, but he couldn't think of where anything could have aroused the man's suspicions, except the part of his being originally Czech, and that had to be done because of his accent. He told himself to take it easy, because there was no reason to think that anything had gone wrong, but his pulse ran quickly and he was aware of prickling tension at the nape of his neck.

Ilona stood at the barred window, biting her lip. She looked young and lovely, with her new raven curls framing her oval face. From somewhere in the prison came a sudden ululating scream, like a sound torn from an animal's throat, thin and faint, and he saw Ilona start and turn pale and bite her lip again. Matyas was scowling. He stood like a dark rock near the door, leaning against the stone wall.

Finally footsteps sounded in the corridor outside, and Durell swung around to face the door. The lieutenant came in. He was not alone. Another man came in behind him, his steps quick and short, almost mincing. Durell looked into the other man's dark, amused eyes, and he felt as if he had been struck a deep and mortal blow. It couldn't be, but it was. He had seen this short, fat little man who looked like some small-time entrepreneur only forty-eight hours ago, across half the world. If he had any doubts, Ilona's quick, shuddering gasp confirmed it.

The other man was Bela Korvuth.

Chapter Seventeen

KORVUTH stood smiling, his hands in the pockets of his blue overcoat, his round face partly shadowed under a broad-brimmed felt hat. His saddle nose looked shiny in the harsh, naked light. The lieutenant stood beside Korvuth with his hand gun drawn.

"So," Korvuth said quietly. "We have both traveled fast and far. It is pleasant to see you again. You too, Ilona."

"You traveled faster than I thought," Durell said.

"All things are possible to a knowledgeable man. Would you prefer that we speak English? The lieutenant here is a good man, but too curious, and this is a matter of grave importance, where loose tongues might upset our plans."

"Did Wyman get word to you about Dr. Tagy?" Durell asked.

"I received word. Have you found the good man?"

"No," Durell said.

"It is the last thread that needs knotting up. And then the matter will be closed. Closed far better than I had hoped. Please stand quite still, Mr. Durell. I have a gun in my pocket. I have only to shout for help, and you three will be destroyed, torn to pieces. You are a bold man but a reckless one. I thought better of you. In our business, Mr. Durell, results are not always founded on a high-spirited bravery such as yours. It is the cool mind, the analytical mind, that succeeds in the end."

Durell's face was a blank mask. There was a sickness writhing in him, a sense of complete and utter defeat, of disaster piling atop other disasters; but nothing showed in his features. He smiled.

"You still don't have Dr. Tagy," he said.

"But you know where he is."

"I told you I didn't."

"You can be persuaded to change your mind. Perhaps Ilona, our clever little girl, can be induced to tell us of your accomplishments." Bela Korvuth's round face hardened, his mouth grew thin, and his eyes were suddenly bright with uncontrollable rage. "You are spies, all of you! Western, imperialist spies, agitators, fascists, inciters of rebellion! I could shoot you now, with all justification, but you will be far more useful to us at the trial being prepared for your boss, General McFee. It will make fine reading for the whole world, will it not? It will prove to the whole world which side sincerely loves peace."

"Your kind of peace is the peace of the grave," Ilona whispered.

Korvuth flicked a glance at her. "You are not frightened, Ilona?"

"I am already dead. There is nothing to fear now."

"You can be persuaded to change your mind. Where is Dr. Tagy?"

"You will have to find him for yourself," the girl answered.

"I think not. I think you will be happy to take me to him."

Durell said suddenly: "We'll talk to Major Ulitzky. Not to you, Korvuth. After all, you are not important. It is the Russians who run things. I will deal with them, not with you."

Korvuth's round eyes became wide. A flicker of anger showed in their pale, opaque surfaces. He looked at the ratty-faced lieutenant, who scowled angrily.

"We are masters in our own land," Korvuth said.

"You delude yourself. Or you believe your own propaganda. You are nothing. A stooge, a puppet on strings, jumping and dancing as your Russian masters bid you to dance."

He had touched a sore spot in the man's vanity. At no time had Durell dared to glance at Matyas, standing bulkily to one side, near the wall. He did not look at Matyas now. He saw Korvuth flush and the man stepped forward, his hand lashing out, striking Durell across the mouth. The blow was hard, snapping Durell's head to one side. Durell pretended to be staggered by the blow. He fell back against the desk, pushing Ilona to the left, out of the way. Korvuth struck him again, a sudden rage in the man, and then Durell heard a flat, meaty sound, like an axblow on flesh. Matyas had taken his cue. Standing immobile, he had attracted little attention from the lieutenant and Bela Korvuth, and he had understood Durell's desperate maneuver. The lieutenant fell, crumpling at the knees, as Matyas stood over him. Instantly Durell straightened, caught at Bela Korvuth's arm, twisting hard, and clapped a hand over the fat man's mouth. He wrenched hard, hauling the AVO man off balance, his feet off the floor. Matyas was coming up fast, the lieutenant's gun in his hand, his wide mouth stretched in a tight, humorless grin.

"Let me kill him," Matyas murmured.

Korvuth squirmed futilely in Durell's grip.

"If he makes one sound," Durell said.

"He will. You don't know him. He will scream—and die."

"Wait," Durell said.

Korvuth was strong, his fat illusory, his body solid and muscular, fighting his grip like a trapped bull. Durell wrenched his arm up higher behind his back. Korvuth tried to bite the hand clamped over his mouth, and Durell drove a knee into the man's spine, felt the shock of the blow as it hit the AVO man, and then struck again, in the same spot. Korvuth slumped forward, his weight heavy and unfeeling in Durell's grip. Durell let him go carefully. Matyas stood over him. The big man was shaking.

"We have to kill him, I tell you."

"That's not our job. We came here for McFee."

"That is hopeless now. We have to get out of here," Matyas said heavily. "Kill him, and let's go."

"Ilona?" Durell asked.

"Let us finish what we came to do," she answered.

"Can you handle Korvuth and the lieutenant?"

"Give me your gun, Matyas," she said.

Durell swung to the big man. "Do you know the way to the special detention cells?"

"Yes, but—"

"Ilona, stay here in this room. Lock the door. If either the lieutenant or Korvuth revives before we get back, hit them again. Keep them out. Can you do it?"

She nodded. "Yes."

"We won't be gone long," Durell said.

He moved out of the room, with Matyas reluctantly pacing beside him. A stairway led downward at the end of the hall, spiraling into the cellars on stone treads. Lights in wire protective baskets in the ceiling guided their way. A smell came up the stairs, compounded of human agony, feces, sweat, stale air, and blood. It's like a charnel house, Durell thought, only the victims are humans, not animals. They passed several solid steel doors. A guard at the end of the corridor was smoking and reading a newspaper. A woman in a uniform, her body fat and gross, was writing at a small desk. Both the guard and the woman stood up.

"The special prisoner," Matyas said. "Bring him up."

"Has the major arrived?" the woman asked.

"He is due in a few minutes. We want things ready."

"We could do the job just as well as he," the woman grumbled. "We don't need them breathing down our necks."

"Do as you are ordered," Matyas said crisply.

The woman got a ring of keys from her desk and tossed them to the guard. "Get him, Joszef." Her eyes were sullen and resentful, ranging from Matyas to Durell. "I doubt if the prisoner can walk."

"He must be made to walk. And talk."

"Damn them all," the woman said.

The guard went off down the corridor, and Durell helped

himself to a cigarette from a pack on the desk. He was thinking of McFee. If McFee were still drugged, in a half-conscious
state, what would he do when he recognized Durell here in
this place? McFee had had no idea that Durell would follow
him to Budapest. He must have put all hope of rescue from
his mind and considered death as his only chance for escape.
If, in his drugged condition, he recognized Durell and gave
any sign of it, everything might still be lost. His mind flicked
back to Ilona, guarding the two men upstairs. She was only
a small girl, hiding fear and tension under a brave front. But
fear was nothing to be scorned. Durell knew fear in himself,
and respected it, knowing that only a fool refused to be
afraid. He dragged hungrily at the cigarette. What was
taking the guard so long? He didn't like the way the fat,
sloppy woman at the desk kept staring at him, her eyes flat,
like dark, ugly stones in the degenerated suet of her face. He
was sweating under his uniform coat. His mouth was dry, and
the Russian cigarette he had taken from the desk tasted
harsh and strong. He crushed it out, and then he heard
footsteps returning from around a corner of the underground
corridor, and then he saw the guard coming back, pushing
McFee ahead of him.

"Help him," Durell said to Matyas.

Matyas went forward. Durell was aware of the fat woman
watching him, rather than the guard and the prisoner. He
kept his face blank, showing nothing of the shock he experienced at the change in Dickinson McFee's appearance
after only forty-eight hours in the hands of the AVO. The
little man looked gaunt and haggard, only a ghost of his
immaculate, spruce self. His eyes were fixed on the stone
floor, concentrating on each step he was forced to take, as
if in fear of falling and what might happen to him at the
hands of the guard if he did. Each second seemed endless
until McFee paused before Durell.

"Here is your man," the guard said.

McFee looked up. His eyes were dull, without luster, scanning Durell's impassive face. Then he smiled.

"Hello," he said in English.

Durell felt the shock of sudden despair.

Then McFee spat in his face.

Afterward, Durell knew that their chance of success had
rested purely in the lap of the gods. He could not have
succeeded without Matyas and Ilona. He could not have won

if Bela Korvuth hadn't reacted to his taunt about Russian control over the operation. And he could not have made his way free if Major Ulitzky's plane had not been delayed by ten minutes. He knew from past experience that luck and chance should have no part in what he had to do, and yet the instincts of a gambler, bred in him by his grandfather's training and his background paid off. There was no objection from either the fat woman or the guard as he wiped Mc-Fee's spittle from his cheek and then suddenly drove his fist into McFee's grinning mouth. The little man crumpled without a sound, his eyes rolling back in his head. The fat woman chuckled. The guard grinned.

"He has spirit, that one."

"It will be broken soon enough," Durell snapped. He swung to Matyas. "Bring him along. Carry him, if you have to."

They went back up the stone stairway to the main floor of the prison. Laughter came from the common room used by the resting guards near the front entrance, and Durell turned aside, walking with an impatient stride to the small chamber where he had left Ilona guarding Bela Korvuth and the lieutenant. There was no sign of alarm, and everything looked all right when he entered. Ilona had her gun pointed at Bela Korvuth, who sat slumped against the wall, his eyes open and fixed viciously on the girl.

Ilona raised her brown eyes to Durell, warm with relief.

"I gave him his choice. Shout and die, or sit quietly and live."

"You will regret it, all of you," Korvuth whispered. "You are insane if you believe you can escape. Perhaps you exult because you have gotten this far. But your joy will change to screams of pain before it is all finished."

"Shut up, you," Matyas growled. He back-handed Korvuth with a swipe of his thick forearm, and Korvuth fell over sidewise, blood gushing from his broken lips. Durell took a handkerchief and tossed it to him.

"Get on your feet. Cover your mouth with that. We're going out of here."

"And him?" Matyas asked, pointing to the ratty-faced lieutenant.

The uniformed man was still unconscious. "Leave him," Durell said.

Matyas jerked Korvuth to his feet. "I don't like it," he grunted. "You don't know this breed. He makes twenty thousand forints a month, and my brother, a refinery worker in Csepel, makes eight hundred. But he is paid so well because they know he is a fanatic, ready to die. It is better if I break his neck."

Durell looked at the chunky AVO man. "We're going to Dr. Tagy. We're taking him out of the country, and we'll take you part of the way with us. If you yell or raise an alarm now, you will be killed. Matyas will do it gladly. It will mean our deaths, too, but then you will never know what happened to Dr. Tagy. This way, if you have confidence in your abilities, you may find a chance to turn the tables on us, after all, once we join the Tagy family. I offer you this hope, because I know your pride and I know your mind. You will come with us on the chance that you can win the whole of the table stakes."

Korvuth nodded, holding the handkerchief to his bloody mouth. His eyes were bright with vicious hatred. "Yes. Of course I will go with you. Dr. Tagy is a prize I want to win."

"Then your only chance for him is if we get out of here."

"I understand. You are a fool, you know."

Durell smiled tightly. "We'll see."

It was done easily, after all. Matyas's uniform and Korvuth's presence lending authority to their progress, opened the gates of Rezd Prison to the night. McFee had recovered well enough to walk slowly between Durell and Ilona. Matyas brought up the rear, behind Korvuth. Nobody stopped them. There were no questions. It was easier to get out, Durell reflected, than to get in. Their car was where they had left it, outside the gate in the barbed-wire fence. Korvuth got in the back with Matyas. Durell helped McFee in, and the little man slumped on the seat between himself and Ilona.

The truck full of soldiers was gone. The two tanks were still on guard duty.

Durell started the car. "Dick, can you hear me?"

McFee made a groaning noise.

"Relax," Durell said. "You're all right now. Understand? You're all right."

"Dreaming . . ." McFee whispered.

Ilona's teeth were chattering. "Please. Let us go. I think I'm going to be sick. I tried hard not to be afraid, but I think if we stay here another moment—"

"All right," Durell said. He was worried about McFee's condition. "We'll go back to town now. We've got a long night ahead of us."

Chapter Eighteen

IT WAS an hour later. Durell sat wearily in Maria's kitchen, a cup of coffee before him, Ilona at his side. Ilona bent forward and kissed him lightly, smiling. "It will be all right, darling. We're all right so far. All that is left is to get out of the city."

There was the sound of sirens in the distance. For the past twenty minutes, Durell knew, every police agency in Budapest had been alerted to look for him. His rescue of McFee from the Rezd Prison had become known, and there had been no chance to get out of the city before the roads were blocked. Not with McFee the way he was. Whatever drugs had been used on him still had a lingering, stupefying effect, and expect for that brief moment of life in the prison when Durell first saw him, McFee had been dull and listless, scarcely able to walk.

Durell looked around the crowded apartment now, wondering what he could do with all these people. Dr. Tagy and his wife, the boy Janos, Maria and Ilona, McFee, Matyas —all their lives were forfeit. How long would it be before the dragnet being cast in every direction by the AVO happened to fall on this place? He couldn't guess how much time he had left. The old Zis sedan was hidden in the alley behind the apartment house, but it could well be suicide to try to use it.

"Sam," Ilona said. "Try to talk to McFee again. We need his help."

"All right."

He got up, conscious of his own physical weariness, the drag on his mind. Maria and the boy, Janos, were guarding Bela Korvuth in the main room of the apartment. Mrs. Tagy and Dr. Tagy were in the bedroom with McFee. Matyas stood outside on the street below as a lookout.

McFee looked bad. His breathing was ragged, his color was gray, and Mrs. Tagy shook her head in answer to Durell's silent inquiry.

"Has the brandy helped?" he asked.

"I could not get him to take any," the woman said. "He thinks it is poison."

135

"He talked to you?"

"Only that. Nothing else."

"Go out and join the others," Durell said. "Leave the brandy here. I want to talk to him alone, please."

The woman hesitated. "How much longer are we to stay here?"

"I don't know," Durell said. "I had hoped to get you out of the city tonight. But I don't know, now."

"Is this man important to you?"

He nodded. "Very important."

"You will not take us unless he can come, too?"

"We'll see," he said. "Please leave us alone for a few minutes."

He closed the door after them and walked back to the bed, staring down at Dickinson McFee's sprawled, thin figure, trying to remember what he knew of the truth serums and will-destroying drugs, and then picked up the brandy and sat down on the bed beside the small man. McFee's eyes remained closed. His breathing was ragged.

"Dick," he said quietly. "General, listen to me. You can hear me, I know. This is Durell. Sam Durell. The Cajun. You're out of the prison and you're safe. Do you understand? I came over to Budapest to get you out, and now you're out of that cell and you're safe, here with me. This is Durell talking to you. I got you away from the AVO. Think about that. You can believe it. Open your eyes and look at me. Take a nip of this brandy. It's not bad stuff. Of course, my old grandpappy down in Bayou Peche Rouge could distil a batch of the smoothest white corn you ever tasted—I'm sure I gave you some last month when we were in Washington— but this brandy isn't too bad, either. Look at me, Dick. It's Durell. Try some of the brandy. You're safe now."

McFee's eyes opened suddenly, gray, murky, uncertain. "What is your—grandfather's name?"

"Jonathan. Grandpappy Jonathan."

"Name of—his boat?"

"The Three Belles, Dick. You can believe me. You can hear me. It's Sam Durell. Come on, look at me. Try some of the brandy."

The little man's eyes were still cloudy, but his hand came up to touch the bottle, and Durell held it for him until he took a small sip, and then another, and then sighed and shuddered.

"It's a trick."

"You didn't look at me. I had to dye my hair, General. It was black, as it should be, until a couple of hours ago. I had to make it blond. That's the trouble, you're just not used to it. Look again."

McFee's eyes focused with an effort on Durell's face. Then his glance went around the room, touching the homey, feminine, pitifully meager appointments Maria Stryzyk had used to decorate it. A look of wonder slowly dawned in his haggard face. "Sam?"

"That's right. Try some more brandy, General. Then try to sit up. I'm going to walk you around. You've had a needle, right? You remember it? You were in prison, but I got you out, and now I need you on your feet to help us get all the way out, free and clear of this mess. Come on, sit up. Stand up. Let's walk a bit."

It was slow, exhausting work, coaxing the man's numbed mind and body back to reality. The brandy helped, and Durell was patient, walking him back and forth in the small bedroom. Time was like a giant clamp, squeezing him with impatience, bringing nearer with every minute the threat of ultimate destruction. Yet he could not hurry his work with McFee. He took it slowly, gently, teasing the man's mind with phrases and memories.

"What happened to your guide Tibor?" he asked once.

"Shot. Dead in a ditch."

"They didn't find him?"

"Don't think so."

"But they got you, eh?"

"The son of a bitch," McFee muttered.

"Who?"

"Who you think? Our own boy. Ratted on us. Tipped them I was coming in."

"Wyman? Roger Wyman?"

"Oh, you met him? Bastard. Dirty, treasonous bastard."

"We'll get him, General. As soon as you can walk, we'll start out. I've got Dr. Tagy and his family with me. I've even got Korvuth—"

It had been quiet in the other room until this moment, with only an occasional murmur of conversation from the others. Now Durell suddenly paused, as something suddenly crashed in there, as if a piece of furniture had been knocked over. Ilona's scream was stifled. There was another crash, and a scuffling of struggling feet, and Durell spun to McFee. "Stay here."

He slammed open the bedroom door and jumped into the other room. It was Bela Korvuth. Somehow he had managed to get Ilona to drop her guard. He had jumped her, upsetting a round pie-crust table, and grabbed the pistol she had been covering him with. He was turning now, his grin tight, his round face suddenly looking drawn and vicious as he spun toward Durell. The Tagys stood in frightened paralysis. Ilona was sprawled on the floor, struggling to rise. A trickle of blood ran down from her newly dyed black hair. And then Durell heard Maria Stryzyk laugh.

"Bela? Look at me, Bela."

She had a kitchen knife in her hand. Her narrow, fanatical face was pale with taut rage.

"You killed my brother. You had no right to kill him, no need to bother Endre. He was out of it, he had quit for good—"

Bela Korvuth made the mistake of changing his target from Durell to the dark-haired woman. Maria moved too fast for Durell to interfere. The knife flashed, the blade flickering in the dim light of the crowded room. Durell heard the chunking sound it made as she drove it home. A look of utter amazement came across Bela Korvuth's face. The assassin whose business it was to kill, to provide death for those he was ordered to kill, looked stunned. The knife was still in Maria's hand. She screamed something and struck again, and then the blade caught in bone and she was unable to keep her grip on the hilt as Korvuth's fall wrenched it free. Maria began cursing and kicking at the body, and Durell caught her thin form and flung her aside and then bent to help Ilona.

"Are you all right?"

"Yes, he tried . . . I'm sorry, I was careless, I looked at Dr. Tagy for a moment instead of keeping my eyes on him."

"Maria?"

The woman said breathlessly: "I'm not sorry. I'd do it again. I wish I could. I wish I could kill him over and over again . . ." Her voice spiraled upward, nearing hysterics, shrill and loud in the narrow room. Durell slapped her, hard. Her head rocked back and a strangled sound moved in her throat, and then she swallowed and leaned back against the wall and then sank slowly to a sitting position on the floor, as if her legs could no longer support her. She began to laugh softly and rock back and forth, hugging herself, never taking her eyes off the dead man.

"No one will weep for that man," Ilona whispered.

Durell turned and looked at McFee in the bedroom doorway. McFee's eyes were clear and bright.

Durell caught Janos Tagy's shoulder and pushed the boy toward the front door of the apartment. "Go down and get Matyas. We'll need him. We've got to pull out of here. Somebody must have heard Maria scream."

The boy nodded and ran out of the room. Durell went and got the brandy bottle and forced a drink between Maria's clenched teeth. The woman coughed and sputtered, then laughed softly. "It was for Endre . . ."

"I know. We should thank you. He could have ruined us all."

"I didn't do it for you. I did it for Endre."

Durell turned away from her and looked at Dr. Tagy. "Do you think you can travel now, Doctor?"

"If I must, I can. It will be better if we leave now."

Then Janos came back into the room. His face was white. "Matyas isn't downstairs on guard any more. He's gone." Janos swallowed. "And so is the car."

The street was dark and cold. Only a few lights shone in the tall windows of the old stone houses that had been converted to apartments, and there was a bright street light at the corner down the hill, where the trolley line came up from the center of Buda. Durell had checked the back alley to make sure that Matyas hadn't simply moved the car a little farther away from the house. It wasn't in sight. The others were waiting for him in the dark courtyard behind the apartments. There was no sign of anything suspicious. Perhaps Matyas had simply changed his mind and decided to stay in Budapest; but Durell could not accept that, after the man's help in the Rezd Prison. Matyas, as well as he, was a marked man.

He heard the sound of a motor grinding up the hill, and paused to watch and wait. The motor was too heavy and strong for a passenger car, yet it did not seem like that of a truck, either. Headlights swung around the corner, and in the glare of the street lamp over the trolley stop, Durell saw it was an old yellow bus. The body of the bus was dark, and it did not seem to be carrying any fares. It came up the hill slowly, the motor straining, and for a moment the headlights caught Durell in the doorway where he watched. The lights blinked off for a moment, then came on again. Durell suddenly stepped forward, recognizing inspiration. He waved his arm, and the bus came to a halt, and Matyas leaned down from the high window of the driver's seat. The man's broad, dark face was grinning, his teeth agleam in the dim light.

"Hello! Were you worried about me?"

"A little. Where did you get that?"

"The bus? Oh, I stood out here thinking," Matyas said, with a great show of being casual, although he looked very pleased with himself. "We're quite a crowd by now, and the car is hot, as you would say. So I thought of a friend of mine who drives this bus for the city administration, and I thought of how fine a vehicle it would be for us, so I drove the old car of Janos's down to the terminal garages and saw my friend. It was easy to convince him to yield the keys and keep his mouth shut. He thinks I've graduated from my AVO uniform to plainclothes."

"Hold it right there," Durell said.

Turning, he ran back to the alley where the others were huddled in a dark, shivering group. Quickly he organized them and one by one they slipped through the shadows and boarded the waiting bus.

"What about our friend Bela?" Matyas asked.

"He's dead. He tried to break things up, and Maria killed him."

Matyas looked at the dark, thin woman with admiration. "Now that is what I call a real woman. One who is not afraid, who can act with speed and decision. Come sit by me, Maria. We can talk together on the way."

McFee signaled to Durell from the back of the bus, and as it lurched forward on the beginning of what was to be a memorable journey, Durell took the Russian rifle from Janos and worked back to join the little man.

"I don't know how to thank you, Sam," McFee said tiredly.

"We're not out of the woods yet."

"I know that. In a way, I ought to bat your ears down for coming in after me. It was a crazy thing to do. On the other hand, I'm grateful. I don't know how long I could have held out against them. I don't think they were really sure of my identity, or they would have really put the screws on me, and I lost my pills, so I couldn't put myself out of their reach. I guess I'm a bit too old for this sort of thing, after all."

"You gave me a free hand," Durell said. "I thought it best to come this way."

"Do you think we can make it?"

Durell looked at Matyas up in the driver's seat; the big man was talking happily to Maria, who sat listening quietly and smiling. "I begin to think so," he said softly. "With these people, anything is possible. They want freedom in a way we've almost forgotten, General. Maybe they'll be good for us. They'll remind us of some things we take for granted, which we can lose too easily if we don't stay sharp about it."

McFee sighed. He looked very tired. "But there will always be people like Roger Wyman."

"He's our only loose end. We'll tie him up," Durell said. "You'd better try to rest now. We may have a long way to walk, later on."

The bus was already in the outskirts of Buda, rolling westward on the highway. The night was dark and windy and cold, with no stars, and every now and then a spit of rain sprayed the wide windows of the vehicle. Durell started forward to talk to Matyas about the route he was taking, and Ilona plucked at his sleeve and he sank down into the seat beside her. She smiled at him, a wistfulness on her small, pretty face, and then she turned her head so she wasn't looking directly at him. Her hands were restless in her lap.

"Everything has been moving so fast, Sam. You and I have not had a moment alone since those hours in Hegedus's farm. Yet I have been thinking of you constantly. You're on your way home, at last."

"So are you," Durell said. "You're coming with us, all the way."

"I don't know. I can't make up my mind about it."

"You can't stay here in Hungary."

"Probably not. It is just a feeling I have. As if I were deserting people who need help so desperately."

"You've done your share," Durell said. "Don't think about it."

"Who is to measure the cup and say it is full now, there is enough given to it, you may rest and drink?"

"You're tired," Durell said. "Tomorrow it will look different to you."

"Tomorrow you will be flying back to Deirdre," she said.

"I haven't thought about her."

"Yes, you have. You have never forgotten her and you never will. What happened between us was nothing. Only a moment of hysteria on my part, a moment of loneliness for you. There is no need to reproach yourself about it. I have no regrets. I shall always be grateful to you."

Durell leaned forward and kissed her lightly. Her lips were cool and unresponsive. She touched his cheek with light, slim fingers.

"I want to sleep now," she said.

Chapter Nineteen

THE FIRST BARRICADE showed up in the village of Rozsa-domb, in the outskirts of Budapest. A truckload of soldiers stood at the intersection of the secondary road Matyas had taken. In the bus, everything was dark and quiet, and Durell had ordered everyone to sit quietly in their seats as if they were ordinary passengers. A Russian sub-lieutenant with a machine gun halted the bus and climbed aboard, his slanted Mongolian eyes glittering and suspicious. The man spoke only a few words of halting Hungarian, and it was obvious, from his lack of ease, the manner in which his eyes touched the appointments of the bus interior, and his general air of nervousness, that he was not long from the wild steppes of Central Asia. In some respects he was all the more to be feared, Durell thought quietly, leaning his head back against the seat as if weary of delays and wishing only sleep. Beside him, under the fold of his coat, was the automatic rifle, his finger on the trigger. The sub-lieutenant swaggered through the bus, barked something at Matyas, who shrugged expressively, and then climbed down again and waved them through.

When the trucks were out of sight, Durell got up and sat behind Matyas. "What did he say to you?"

"He wanted to know where we were going." Matyas laughed softly. "I told him this was an express bus to Györ. And that is not far from the truth, is it?"

"You won't be able to use that when we come to an AVO check point."

"I know where they usually put up their blockades. We can take some side roads to get around them into the country-side. But there will be more Russians up ahead, in tanks. I I know them well, the dirty savages."

In twenty minutes they reached a second roadblock. Again it was manned by Russians, this time in armored cars, with the dark masses of T-54's bulking in the shadows under a grove of trees flanking the road. The same routine was followed. Matyas was a consummate actor. He expressed indignation, impatience at his loss of time on the schedule he was supposed to follow, and just the right amount of respectful cooperation toward the Soviet military. They were passed through.

"Now we will turn north," Matyas said, grinning. "There are a number of secondary roads we can take."

"If we run into a check point on them, won't it arouse suspicion because the bus belongs on the main highway?" Durell asked.

"I can always say I was detoured at the last barricade. And I shall complain bitterly about it."

"If we have a straight run, how long will it take to reach the border?"

Matyas shrugged. "Two, closer to three, hours. With luck." He sighed. "But we do not have a straight run. We will go north of Győr on this road I know, and then cut west again. It will be all right."

"Make it three hours, then," Durell said.

"If we are lucky, yes."

Durell went back in the rocking bus and sank wearily into the leather seat next to Ilona. She was smoking a cigarette, staring out through the wide windows at the dark, flickering countryside. They were well out of the city now, following a graveled road that twisted and turned like a snake through small hills and dense patches of woodland. Here and there a dim light flickered from some peasant's farmhouse. The bus jounced wildly over ruts in the road, the springs squealing in protest as Matyas pushed down on the gas with abandon. Durell leaned across the girl to take her cigarette, and saw the silver streaks of tears on her face.

"What is it?" he whispered. "Why are you crying, Ilona."

"I don't know."

"There must be a reason."

"I'm a fool. I feel confused."

"What about?"

"You. I think I'm in love with you, darling."

He said nothing and she turned, her dark hair glinting in the faint starshine that came through the bus windows. She smiled weakly and touched his hands. "I'm afraid I made a bad bargain with you, after all," she said quietly. "You are disappointed in me now, aren't you?"

"No, but—"

"You need not say anything about it. It's all right. I know you don't love me. And that is not the whole cause for the way I feel. I just don't know if I'm doing the right thing, going back with all of you."

"You can't stay in Hungary," he said flatly.

"But I want to. I feel—like a coward, running away."

"You're not a coward. Don't think about it."

She looked at him with solemn eyes. "Tell me, truly. Aren't you afraid, sometimes, in the work you do, that you may be making a wrong decision, taking a step in the wrong direction?"

"I try not to think about it."

"Very well. I'll try not to think, too."

It was cold in the bus. The heating equipment did not operate satisfactorily, and the silent passengers sat huddled in their seats, uncomfortable and tense. Durell spoke to Dr. Tagy, then Maria, then went back to McFee. McFee had the Russian sub-machine gun in his lap.

"We've been too lucky," McFee said. "We'll have trouble soon."

"The longer it's postponed, the better, and the closer we get to the border."

"Do you honestly think we're going to make it, Cajun?"

Durell thought of the busload of people depending on him. The responsibility weighed on him with tangible pressure, like a load on his back. "We'll make a good try at it."

"We can't afford to be captured again, Sam."

"I know that."

"Some of these people will talk about us, if they're taken, too."

"I know."

"We can't let that happen, Sam."

Durell looked at the little man's face in the shadows of the bus seat. McFee's meaning was clear enough. They either won through to freedom for all of them, or they had to die. Everyone in the bus. There was no other choice possible.

"Do you understand, Sam?"

Durell looked at the automatic in McFee's hands. McFee had taken up a position in the very last seat in the bus, where his gun covered the nodding heads of their passengers. He looked especially at Ilona.

"Let's not borrow trouble, Dick."

"I just wanted you to know what I'll have to do, Sam. You can take care of Ilona, if you prefer."

"I couldn't kill her," Durell said. "That's nonsense."

"You'll have to, if we're caught. Otherwise, I'll do it." McFee's words were quiet, and terrible because of the calm riding behind his narrow face. "She's in love with you, Sam."

"I know. She told me."

"How do you feel about it?"

"I don't feel anything about it. You're still borrowing trouble. We're halfway to the border already."

"Halfway isn't good enough," McFee said. "Go on back and hold her hand."

An hour went by. Most of the people in the bus sat unmoved, waiting for disaster. The boy, Janos, wanted to relieve Matyas at the wheel, but the big man pushed him aside. The road they followed with the ponderous vehicle was little more than a country lane, muddy, filled with ice and slippery when they went through the deep shadows of wooded territory. Once, Durell saw flares lifting in the horizon of the night sky, far to the south. Budapest was far behind, and if they had been on the main highway to the west, they would be close to the border by now. But the roadblocks on the main highway would have been death traps, each one of them, and it was better not to push their luck too far. He only hoped that Matyas was as good as his word and knew his way along these back roads. If they got lost and were forced to waste precious hours wandering around, the night would be gone, and in daylight escape would be impossible.

Matyas called him forward finally, and Durell went down the aisle of the bus to sit directly behind the driver's seat. Matyas spoke soberly. "This is as far as I can go, staying off the main roads. In about three more miles, we come out on a main highway going west. There is no other route we can take, you understand? There will be a roadbock in a short distance, once we reach the highway, and it will be manned by Hungarian AVO people. It will be the point of greatest danger for us."

"How far are we from the frontier now?"

"When we reach the block, it will be about ten miles."

"How much speed can you get out of the bus?"

"Fifty—maybe sixty miles an hour."

"We may have to break through and push for it," Durell said. "Be ready, if it comes to that."

"Yes. There will be much shooting, if we do that, though. And the women will be in danger."

Durell looked back and saw McFee on the rear seat, with his gun. "We'll all be in danger. The women take equal chances with the men in this."

"I don't like to do that," Matyas said. "Maria and I—"

"You take your chances together."

"All right. Here we go."

The bus bounced and rocked on the rough unpaved road for another quarter-mile, and then abruptly lifted with a jolt onto concrete paving. Matyas turned left. The highway was broad and smooth and ominously empty. Durell knew that the town of Györ was behind them now, and no alert guard would be fooled by the sudden appearance of a wandering bus from Budapest. He felt tension creep along his nerves and muscles as the bus headlights swept the concrete ribbon ahead.

The barrier showed up quickly enough. A glow of light appeared, brightening steadily as Matyas headed for it without slackening speed. A red flare shot up into the sky, and other spotlights suddenly came on, flooding the area ahead with vivid brightness. There were several guard huts visible, flanking the highway, a wooden and steel barricade, the looming monstrous shapes of more Russian tanks, and then the figures of several men standing with rifles ready, waving them down.

"Slow down and stop," Durell ordered.

Matyas thinned his mouth. "It is a temptation to crash through."

"It wouldn't work. Stop and go through the same routine. Say you are lost, that you were detoured, as you planned to say before."

Matyas touched the brakes and the bus slowed its wild pace. The bright island of light around the roadblock came swimming up out of the dark pattern of the night, seeming to rush toward them out of black space. Matyas braked again. Air hissed and rubber squealed on the concrete. Durell heard a flat cracking sound, and he wondered if a warning shot had been fired at them, and then Matyas had the bus halted and a uniformed AVO man came walking angrily across the road as Matyas opened the doors.

This time it was a captain, and he was backed up by half a dozen armed men near the guard huts, as well as the glinting muzzles of tank weapons in the shadows of the highway shoulders. Ahead, the highway swept in a long, gentle curve to the south and west, and the dark shape of more woodland loomed against the night. The AVO captain came aboard with a Mauser pistol in his hand. He looked angry and suspicious, barking swift questions at Matyas while his eyes raked the dim interior of the bus. He looked dangerous.

"Who are you people? Stand up and get out of this bus. I want to look at you all."

The AVO captain was squat and powerfully built, with a pock-marked face and a swaggering stride. Matyas said something to him in a placating voice, but the man spit on the bus floor and walked down the aisle straight toward Ilona.

"This one," he said, looking down at her. "I think I know you, don't I? Stand up, girl, and let's have a good look." He swung angrily. "The rest of you, get out of the bus! This is as far as you go. Get your papers ready and walk over to the hut, into the light."

This was it, Durell thought. There was no escape, no chance of bluffing. The man was already suspicious, arrogant, sensing something wrong about the bus wandering the highway in the night. Durell stood up and nodded slightly to Matyas, who sank back in his driver's seat behind the wheel. The diesel engine was still running, idling throatily. Ahead were the steel and wood barricades, the dim shapes of tanks like primordial monsters sheltering in the darkness under the trees.

"Leave the girl alone," Durell said to the AVO man.

"You give me a suggestion?" The squat man spun in the aisle, his gun up. But he made the mistake of looking back through the open door of the bus, where his men were waiting, smoking and talking. It was enough for Durell. Ilona dropped away as he struck at the man's gun, knocking it down, catching the man's arm and slamming it hard over the brass-trimmed edge of Ilona's seat. The Mauser exploded with a shattering crash, punching a slug into the floor of the bus. At the same moment, Matyas clashed gears and tramped on the gas pedal. The bus lurched ahead with a sudden roar of the engine. Durell was prepared for the movement; the AVO captain was not. Durell struck hard again, the edge of his palm clipping the thick nape of the man's neck. The AVO captain fell, lurching, and his head struck the back of Ilona's seat. At the same moment, the bus slammed at rising speed into the barrier ahead. Wood splintered, steel screeched, glass shattered. Durell was thrown from his feet, caught a grip on the seat, and stumbled over the AVO man. The Mauser slid along the bus aisle and he caught it up, pulling himself to his feet.

Everything was confusion. He heard the yells of alarm from the guards, and a machine gun on one of the tanks began to stutter and more glass flew in wicked, lethal shards as slugs came through the bus windows.

"Down!" Durell yelled. "Everybody down, on the floor!"

The motion of the bus was insane, rocking crazily but still going forward, dragging part of the barricade along with it, the lumber and steel screeching on the concrete. Someone fell on Durell and he pushed angrily, struggling up. They were still moving. Janos grabbed his arm and babbled something and he shook the boy free and staggered forward to Matyas. The big man still clung to the wheel. One half of the big windshield was shattered, and blood streamed down the man's face from a deep gash across his forehead.

"My eyes," he gasped. "I can't see."

Durell braced himself against a steel hand pole and got out a handkerchief and dabbed at Matyas's face, wiping the blood away. "Keep going."

"The tanks will follow."

"Can they catch us?"

Matyas shook his head. "They can do forty. As long as they don't blow our tires, we're all right."

Durell looked back. A blinding, iridescent glare filled the rear windows of the rocking bus as a spotlight centered on them. They were already twenty, thirty yards away from the check point, leaving it fast. He saw men running, saw the angry spit of exhaust from tank engines as the T-54's started up. There came a sound like a clap of thunder, a muzzle flare, and the screech of a shell going by. The tank men were using their 75's, hoping to hit the bus. But the road curved, and although Matyas was having trouble controlling the vehicle, they were sliding around the long curve to the south and west, putting trees between them. The speedometer needle was creeping up, past fifty, sixty kilometers, wavering crazily.

"You'll have to go faster," he shouted.

Matyas nodded, and Durell gave him his handkerchief to wipe off the blood that ran into his eyes. Another machine gun began firing at them, and four or five slugs struck the back of the bus, screaming angrily, and more glass shattered. Someone screamed. A spotlight flickered past them, caught them, bathed the inside of the bus with eerie bright radiance. To Durell's quick glance, it looked like a shambles. He sought out Ilona and saw her taking the gun from McFee and poking the muzzle through the shattered rear window. She fired rapidly, in quick bursts, and the spotlight abruptly went out.

Durell worked his way back to her. "Are you all right?"

"Yes. It was Mrs. Tagy who screamed."

Durell swung back and saw Dr. Tagy holding his gray-haired wife. Janos was tearing his shirt into strips for bandaging.

"It was flying glass," Dr. Tagy said. "She will be all right."

Durell stumbled over the AVO man, knelt, lifted the man's head and shoulders. He looked unconscious, possibly dead. One of the bullets had hit him high in the chest. He dropped the man, looking for Maria, didn't see her, then went forward and found her crouching behind Matyas's driver's seat. She was trying to keep the blood from Matyas's wound from interfering with the big man's vision. Her smile was quick as she saw Durell.

"No casualties?"

"None yet."

"If we can keep them behind us for fifteen minutes . . ."

Durell nodded and looked back. Headlights from the pursuing tanks were still visible on the road behind them, but thanks to the curve of the highway, the slight rise and dip of the gently rolling hills, the tanks hadn't used their cannon after the first wild shots. He felt the bus tremble and a quick, rhythmic jolt set his teeth to chattering, and he knew that one of the dual rear tires had gone flat. It was not the tanks behind them that worried him now. He knew that the radio had already jumped ahead of them to the frontier, sounding the alarm, alerting machines and men and guns to stop them.

He looked at his watch. Five minutes had gone by since they had crashed through the roadblock. It was enough to give them a safe lead from motorcycles, trucks or cars that might give chase. The danger from the rear was gone. What lay ahead looked dark, a gamble against the biggest odds he had ever chosen. He could count somewhat on the enemy's confusion. Ten minutes might not be enough time for them to organize an airtight blockade of the road. But it wasn't good enough. He couldn't depend on that. Turning, he worked his way down the bus aisle, grabbing handholds as the bus lurched crazily, his feet crunching on broken glass. He crouched beside Matyas at the wheel. Maria was still working on the wound on the man's head.

"How much farther?" Durell asked.

"Five miles, maybe."

"What have they got up ahead?"

Matyas shrugged. His face looked gray and bleak in the dim light from the instrument panel. "Too much, maybe."

"You don't think we can crash through?"

"They will be ready now. Guns, mines, tank traps. We can only try."

"You'd better slow down, then," Durell said.

"What?"

"Look for a side road. Bear north."

"They will all be the same, friend. The border area is closed tight."

"But they'll be looking for us on the highway. They won't expect this bus to go anywhere else. Take any road, no matter how bad it is. Push ahead until we can't go any farther."

"And then?"

"We'll try to walk out," Durell said quietly.

Their chance came sooner than he had hoped. A narrow cut appeared in the woods lining the highway up ahead, and Matyas slammed on the brakes, heaving at the clumsy bus wheel to make the turn. For a moment Durell thought they were going to turn over as the floor lifted under him. Branches crashed against the roof of the bus. The road was nothing but a frozen mud lane boring like a tunnel through the woods. The heavy wheels broke through the frozen surface and began to spin crazily, and the bus slid sidewise toward a parallel ditch. Matyas grunted and clung to the big wheel. Mrs. Tagy made a whimpering sound in the back of the bus. The wheels slid a few more feet, than gained traction and the bus lurched ahead, down the twisting, narrow lane away from the highway.

Durell drew a deep breath and looked back. Faint headlights flickered through the trees on the main road behind them, and he reached across Matyas and flicked off the headlights. Instantly Matyas took his foot off the gas as the way ahead was plunged into darkness. Yet enough light came from the pursuing tanks on the highway to guide them safely, at a snail's pace, along the rutted dirt road. The tank headlights speared through the woods in long, ghostly streamers, flickering over and beyond them, and then were gone.

"Can you see your way?" Durell asked.

Matyas nodded. "Just about."

"How far do we have to go?"

"Maybe five miles, if the road goes that way."

They went ahead cautiously, the bus lunging like a crippled monster through the brush and weeds. Now and then they crossed a small wooden bridge, edging carefully over the gap until they reached the hard terrain on the other side. The landscape began to change after a few minutes, flattening and lowering into the swamps and marshes that characterized the frontier land. There were no stars and no moon, and in the hollows, the white frozen mist was forming. The inside of the bus was very cold. Now and then as the road led them into hollows, the mist was too heavy for any visibility at all, and Matyas had to turn on the dim lights for brief moments.

Durell looked at his watch. They were ten minutes off the highway, then fifteen. The lane was degenerating rapidly into two ruts across the frozen swamp. The mist was heavier, then it cleared, and to the left loomed the sudden, ominous outline of a spidery watch tower. Matyas kept going in low gear. The grinding of the laboring motor seemed enormously loud. There was no sign of life from the tower, but Durell knew better than to hope they might elude the listening ears and prowling patrols in this territory. He felt tension build inside him, and he started back down the aisle in the center of the bus, getting everyone ready to debark for the last dash on foot for the frontier line.

There was no warning when they hit the land mine.

Durell heard the blast only as a dim, echoing concussion after the sheet of flame that lifted the front end of the bus several feet into the air. It was followed by another as the momentum of the vehicle carried the front wheels onto a second mine. He was aware of cries and screams and rumbled curses from Matyas, the shattering of glass and the tortured sound of twisting metal, and then he felt the blow of the explosion like a giant's hand slammed across his chest and he watched the front windshield cave in toward him as he fell back.

Chapter Twenty

FLAMES crackled nearby, and Durell pushed himself up, seeing the lurid red that outlined the misty swamp all around him. Someone spoke to him quickly, soothingly. It

was Ilona. He stared at the bus and saw that the front end
was twisted and smoking, the entire vehicle atilt on its left
side, windows shattered, burning fiercely. From far in the
distance came the stuttering of a machine gun. The wheels
of the bus were still turning slowly and he knew he had
blacked out for only a few moments, but he could not remember getting out of the bus or what had happened to the others.
He pushed himself erect, swaying, and Ilona stood up with
him, her dark hair, cut in the Italian-boy style she had chosen,
glinting with reflected coppery flames.

"Where is everybody?"

"McFee took them on ahead. Into the swamp. I stayed
with you. We must hurry," Ilona said.

"Who was hurt?"

"Matyas. And Maria."

"Bad?"

"Matyas is dead," she said.

Durell felt a deep, swift pang of bitter regret. "And Maria?"

"She was falling in love with him. She took McFee's
'guitar.' She went off toward the watch tower. It is her gun
you hear. She will hold off the guards. But please hurry,
darling. We must go after the others."

Durell nodded. He took a few uncertain steps and then he
felt steadier and stronger. He began walking at a rapid pace
through the swamp with the girl. The fog was like a shroud
all around them, and he could not see or hear the others
ahead of them. Now and then they stumbled through icy
water that was knee deep, numbing his feet and ankles. He
trusted Ilona to choose the right direction, and she seemed to
go ahead with assurance, confident of her way.

There was no sign of the rutted lane they had been following in the bus, but there was sporadic firing to the left, where
he had glimpsed the watch tower, and he wondered about
Maria and then he hoped McFee was leading the Tagy family
in the right direction, too. He kept the Mauser in his hand,
but the mists closed off everything within a radius of twenty
feet as they stumbled on.

Once Ilona fell and he helped her up and they struggled
on, and then she fell again and he made her sit on a fallen
log to rest and catch her breath. For the moment, the swamp
shrouded in its white, frozen mist was utterly silent.

She was breathing raggedly and she leaned her weight
against him. "I am worried about the others."

"McFee will see them safely across."

"There will be patrols. We are near the canal again, and I don't think it will be frozen over enough for them to walk across. They will have to wade, and with this alarm out for us, there will be guards watching for us. They have seen the burning bus by now. There will be a hundred men around us in a few more minutes."

He looked at the white fog to the west. The brittle reeds of the marsh grass stood higher than his head, and he remembered the tales of refugees who had tried to cross this swamp without a guide and become lost and wandered for hours and even for days without finding their way to safety. The girl's breath made a fine vapor in the frosty air, and she reached for his hand, leaning heavily against him.

"Come, we must go on, darling. I will take you to the canal."

"And no farther?" he asked.

"I have been confused, but things are clearer for me now. My place is not in America. It is here, where I can do some good and help my people. I do not like to think of living with myself as a coward, knowing how I might have helped others in my own country."

He shook his head. "It will be too dangerous for you."

"I think I can manage to stay alive and safe. You should not have any cause to worry about me, Sam. I can keep my hair dark, like this. You like it, don't you?"

"Yes, Ilona."

"Because it reminds you of Deirdre." She touched his face with cold, light fingers. "You do not have to keep the truth from me. You want to go back to her, you want to have her, much more than you ever wanted me. This is the kind of thing a woman knows, without words."

"Is that why you don't want to go back?" he asked quietly.

"No. I told you the main reason. The other—about you, and the way I love you—it would not be fair to either of us if I went with you and became a burden to you."

"You would never be that," he insisted.

"I know. But when you see her again, everything will be different. I am sure of that. She will understand."

"I don't think so," Durell said.

"You will see. I know these things better than you. I wish it could have been different, but some things are not for me, and you must not worry about me when I leave you. I will be all right. Not like Maria, who is bitter and reckless and wants to die. Perhaps she has died already, back there, fighting like a man to give us these few moments to get ahead of the guards. I will not be like that. I will be careful. And useful. You will hear from me again." She stood up. "Come. It is only a little farther to go now."

Ten minutes later they stood at the edge of the swamp. There was no more firing from the south now, where Maria had gone to hold off the guards posted at the watch-tower station. The night was still, with no wind at all, and the mist hung in long, low streamers over the canal ahead that marked the frontier. Here and there a clump of white birches stood like up-thrust hands with twisted, grotesque fingers clawing the dark night. Dogs were barking somewhere behind them, where they had left the bus. Durell wondered about McFee and the Tagys. There was no sign of them up and down the canal, although he could not see very far through the mist. He could only hope they had gotten through safely.

About three hundred yards beyond the canal stood a farm-house, windows cheerfully lighted whenever the mist moved aside to permit a glimpse of the yellow light. Over there was Austria and freedom. Here was tyranny and death.

"Come across with me, Ilona. You can't stay in this area tonight."

The barking of the dogs was louder behind them. "Perhaps you are right. For tonight, anyway."

"Here, let me carry you."

"No, no. I can wade across myself."

The water was bitterly cold, knee-deep in most places, although halfway across the canal Ilona suddenly stepped into a hole and went in above her waist. They were trying to be silent, but she made an involuntary sound of fright when her footing slipped. Durell grabbed for her and caught her close to him, and then a gun cracked behind them and a man's harsh shout of warning broke the silence of the night. Durell looked back. The figures of a dozen men were emerging from the wall of swamp reeds behind them. Dogs ran ahead to the water's edge, barking frantically. A spotlight flared from the watch tower, but the shaft of light was diffused by the mist, making strange iridescent haloes and patches of multi-colored light where the spot wandered.

"Come on," Durell gasped.

He grabbed at Ilona's hand and half dragged her to the opposite bank of the canal. She fell again, and he got an arm around her waist and hauled her out of the water with one last effort. Her teeth chattered and she gasped for breath. A volley of rifle shots followed them, and bullets spanked the frozen embankment of the canal. Durell crouched low and pushed Ilona over the top. The spotlight touched them, swept on, came back and pinned them against the dark earth.

"Run!"

A machine gun chattered. Durell threw the girl to the hard ground after they had gone only a few steps, and fell on top of her. The bullets screamed over their heads. Durell stared ahead. The farmhouse seemed an infinite distance away. The frontier guards were wading into the canal now, close behind them. He crawled forward over the frozen earth, pulling the girl with him. There was a small hut ahead, but Ilona drew him aside when he started for it.

"Not there. We are still in Hungary! Another hundred feet, straight ahead!"

Birch trees stood in eerie clumps to their left. Durell drew a deep breath and gathered himself for a final dash. His heart was pounding.

"Let's go."

They got up and ran. Most of the guards were wading across the canal at the moment, and were unable to fire. But the machine gun promptly began to clatter, and the spotlight sought them out again. The birches came closer, closed around them, were behind them. The farmhouse was near. Three people were standing there, looking at them, beckoning them on. Durell saw they were two men and a woman, and one of the men wore the uniform of an Austrian frontier guard. He saw a small road, a line of telephone poles going westward, and faintly heard the encouraging shouts of the Austrians.

Then Ilona suddenly stumbled and fell.

Instantly he turned and dropped beside her. The girl's face was a tortured white mask upturned to his. She reached back and touched her leg.

"It's a bullet. I can't—you go ahead. Please, please!"

He wasted no time arguing with her. A car was approaching the farmhouse along the road from Austria. He could see the headlights clearly. The first of the AVO men were clambering out of the frozen waters of the canal, running across the dark field toward the birches that hid them. Without wasting another moment, Durell picked up the girl and ran at a staggering gait toward the farmhouse. For an instant she struggled, crying out for him to forget about her and save himself. She was surprisingly light in his arms. He saw a wire fence, broken down into the brittle weeds, and he clambered across and knew at once that he was over the frontier line when faint cheers came from the people at the farmhouse. But there was no safety yet. He knew that the AVO men in desperation might still pursue them.

"Put me down. Please," Ilona whispered.

He ignored her. He was through the fence and somehow still going, and when he looked back, he saw that the AVO men had slowed their pace at last. The machine gun was silent, in the face of the Austrian frontier guard who was coming toward them across the distant field.

It was then that Durell noticed the car again. It had been approaching along the Austrian road to the farmhouse, but now its headlights swung and began to bounce as the driver cut abruptly across the flat field toward them. Durell halted. He was still a hundred yards or more from the farmhouse, and the people there stood waiting for him. He looked back. The AVO men had halted, too. The car's headlights came directly toward him, bathing him in light. Some sixth sense gave him warning, and he knelt and carefully put Ilona down. Her arms clung to him for a moment, and then she let go. Durell straightened with the Mauser in his hand.

The car was a small Italian Topolino. He recognized it. It belonged to the traitor, Roger Wyman.

The Topolino came bouncing across the rough field to within a few feet of them and then stopped. The headlights were switched off and the man inside got out. It was Wyman.

He stood tall and casual, smiling as he came toward them. He did not look like a traitor, a man who had betrayed them to the AVO and done everything he could to insure their capture and death. He looked like any other well-dressed, powerfully built American, his blond hair thick as he took off his little fuzzy Austrian hat. His Nebraska twang sounded like home.

"I see you made it. Congratulations, Durell."

He held out his left hand. His right hand was in the pocket of his tweed overcoat. Durell saw the glint of his white, even teeth in the gloom, saw the hard pale stare of his eyes as he looked at Ilona, sitting on the frozen earth holding her wounded leg.

"How did you get here?" Durell asked.

"We heard at the Embassy that something was breaking

along this section of the frontier. A lot of extra guards, some tanks. Our information service is quite adequate, you know."

"Yours, especially. Get out of my way."

Wyman said smoothly, "Don't point that gun at me, Durell. I have one of my own. I suppose you've guessed that."

"I've figured out a lot of things," Durell said. "Turn around."

"On the contrary. It's you who must turn around. Start walking east. Both of you. They're waiting for you over there in Hungary."

It was a stand-off. The people at the farm had no inkling of what was happening; they still stood in the doorway of the farmhouse, watching, expecting them to turn and walk toward them any moment. The white mist moved around them with long, cold fingers.

Ilona said thinly: "You would make us go back there, Mr. Wyman? To have them kill us?"

"Precisely." Wyman's white teeth gleamed again. "You know where my sympathies lie. It is a matter of reward, of pay. I never had much money, you know. Just a poor farm boy, kicked around from pillar to post. You try to make a gentleman out of yourself, but it never works. You're never accepted, you see. Talk about equality and justice and opportunities! I've been stuck here without advancement for years. The other side offered me plenty, and I don't feel I owe any allegiance to the side that kicks me, sneers at me, insults me."

"You must be crazy," Ilona whispered. "You expect to have things handed to you? You feel bitter because you had to struggle as a boy, getting where you are now? Have you no idea what life means over there?"

"I'm only interested in the dough. And a future with everything money can bring. Come on, get up. That nosy Austrian guard will come over in a minute and see what's keeping us. Go on, get up."

"She can't walk," Durell said. "She's got a bullet in her leg from your friends."

"Help her, then. And drop your gun, please. You can't possibly raise it in time to shoot me before I get you through my pocket. You know the odds, Durell."

"One thing," Durell said. "The people you let slip through the screening apparatus. Bela Korvuth's ring. You know all their names?"

"Of course." Roger Wyman still smiled. "Come along,

now. Help the girl up. You know enough to be sensible, I'm sure."

Ilona said, "Help me, Sam."

He helped her to her feet. She leaned heavily against him. Her face was pale, her eyes not frightened but angry as she looked at Wyman. From the farmhouse came a querulous shout. Ilona spoke quietly.

"How could you, for profit, sell the lives of your fellow countrymen? What do you know about being hurt? You have spent your years feeling sorry for yourself, refusing to accept your own inadequacies, and like a spiteful child, you send better men to their death over there."

"Shut up," Wyman said tightly. "Start walking back. Quickly!"

"No," Ilona said.

She lurched forward against the big blond man, her hand grabbing for the gun in Wyman's hand. At the same moment, Durell jumped for him, driving the girl aside, praying Wyman's gun wouldn't go off. It fired with a shattering burst and Ilona gave a small, choked cry and fell to her knees on the hard turf of the field. The next moment Durell had him, feeling the man's bull-like strength, knowing he was handicapped by the long hours of exhaustion behind him. He couldn't hold Wyman. The gun in the man's hand kept lifting again, the muzzle rising toward him as they grappled. Dimly, Durell heard shouts from the farmhouse and other yells from the AVO men at the frontier line. Wyman's gun crashed again, smashing a bullet into the ground at their feet as they swayed, locked together. Durell hooked his foot behind the other's ankle and suddenly summoned all his remaining energy in the judo maneuver. Wyman was strong, but he was not clever. He lost his balance, went over backward with a curse. His gun hand was wrenched free of Durell's grip and it spit flame wildly as he fired a third time. Ilona screamed. Durell's Mauser slashed across Wyman's face, slashed again, and once more. There was a fury in him beyond his immediate control.

Wyman got to his hands and knees and lurched away to one side. His hands were empty; he had lost his gun. His face streamed blood. Durell drove after him, a lust to kill burning in him. He struck once more and Wyman went down, sprawling on his face in the frozen mud. Durell felt Ilona's hands on him, holding him back. He shook her off, saw her fall, and suddenly the wild anger in him against the man on the

ground began to fade. He straightened, drawing in great,
deep breaths of the freezing night air. Slowly, the roaring
of his pulses began to ease. He saw the Austrian border pa-
trolman help Ilona to stand, and there were other people
running toward him now from the farmhouse. He saw McFee
and Dr. Tagy. They had made it. His anger ebbed still
farther.

"Are you all right, Ilona?"

"Yes. It is just my leg." He saw her wavering smile. "My
return to Hungary will have to be delayed."

Durell touched her cheek with his fingers. He drew another
deep, steadying breath and looked backward at the frontier.
The searchlights in the Hungarian watch tower were going out,
one by one. He heard the dogs barking for another moment,
and then they, too, were silent.

It was over.

McFee came walking across the field toward him. The
small, gray man had deep lines of exhaustion engraved on
his face. He looked at Durell and then at Roger Wyman,
seated on the cold ground.

"I'm glad you didn't kill him, Cajun. We want him back
in Washington. He'll have a lot to tell us."

Durell awoke to bright sunlight streaming through the
windows of his apartment. He had slept for almost twenty-
four hours after the plane landed at the National Airport in
Washington, with Wyman in handcuffs and Dr. Tagy and
his family checked into the Mayflower pending his return
to his laboratories in California with his wife and son. Ilona
had insisted on remaining in Vienna, in the hospital there
after the bullet was removed from her leg. Thinking about
her, Durell could understand why she was adamant about
returning to fight in Hungary's underground for the free-
doms and liberties she was sure would be won eventually. He
remembered the night they shared in the farmhouse attic
with a twist of nostalgic pain that surprised him. He knew
he would probably never see her again. And he remembered
Matyas, driving the bus through that wild ride, and Maria's
tenderness toward him—and her sacrifice that none of them
had witnessed in the swamps around the frontier watch tower.

Durell got out of bed and showered slowly and gratefully,
the hot water soaking the aches and bruises from his long,
lean body. A fresh dressing had been put on his wounded
shoulder, but it was healing well now, and he had no trouble

with it. The telephone rang while he was in the shower, and he didn't bother to answer it. From the windows of his apartment, he could see the top of the Capitol dome and the thin spire of the Washington Monument. This was his home. It was a clear, bright winter day, and the pale sky looked as if it had been scoured clean and new and fresh.

He had never felt so lonely before.

He made his own breakfast, with a pot of Louisiana coffee, and smoked a cigarette and when the telephone rang again, he got up and answered it.

Sidonie Osbourn spoke to him. "Sam? Sam, dear, I'm sorry if I wakened you . . ."

"I'm not coming into the office today," he said.

"There's no need for that. Summerfield got everything we need out of Roger Wyman. The list has been turned over to the FBI. It's within their jurisdiction now. They'll round up the people Wyman let slip into the country. Dr. Tagy and his family have been shipped back to California on this morning's plane . . . Sam, are you listening?"

"Yes," he said. "I'm tired."

"You didn't call Deirdre. I'm phoning from the hospital, by the way."

"I doubt if Dierdre wants me to call her," Durell said.

"Why not come over and see for yourself? McFee has been here. He talked to her for half an hour, told her where you'd been and what you've done. He spoke to her like a Dutch uncle, Sam, dear."

"He had no right—"

"Are you going to be stubborn now, too? She understands now, Sam. She wants to see you, truly. She's being released from the hospital this afternoon, and she wants you to drive her home."

Durell was silent. He looked out through the window at the bright sunlight, and it suddenly seemed brighter, more cheerful. He felt immeasurably better.

He was no longer lonely.

"I'll be right over, Sidonie. And thanks."

"Hurry, dear," she said.

She didn't have to tell him.